ABOVE ALL, DON'T LOOK BACK

CARAF Books

Caribbean and African Literature Translated from French

Carrol F. Coates, Editor

Clarisse Zimra, J. Michael Dash,
and Elisabeth Mudimbe-Boyi,
Advisory Editors

MAÏSSA BEY

ABOVE ALL, DON'T LOOK BACK

Translated by Senja L. Djelouah
Afterword by Mildred Mortimer

University of Virginia Press
Charlottesville and London

Originally published in French as *Surtout ne te retourne pas,*
© 2005 Editions de l'Aube

University of Virginia Press
Translation and afterword © 2009 by the Rector and Visitors of the
University of Virginia
All rights reserved
Printed in the United States of America on acid-free paper

First published 2009

9 8 7 6 5 4 3 2 1

LIBRARY OF CONGRESS CATALOGING-IN-PUBLICATION DATA

Bey, Maïssa.
  Surtout ne te retourne pas. English]
  Above all, don't look back / Maïssa Bey ; translated by Senja L. Djelouah ;
afterword by Mildred Mortimer.
      p.   cm. — (CARAF books: Caribbean and African literature trans-
lated from French)
  Originally published in French as: Surtout ne te retourne pas.
  Includes bibliographical references.
  ISBN 978-0-8139-2843-2 (cloth : alk. paper) — ISBN 978-0-8139-
2844-9 (pbk. : alk. paper) — ISBN 978-0-8139-2850-0 (e-book)
    1. Earthquakes—Algeria—Fiction. 2. Disaster victims—Fiction. 3.
Natural disasters—Psychological aspects—Fiction. 4. Natural disasters—
Social aspects—Fiction. I. Djelouah, Senja L. II. Title.
  PQ3989.2.B477S8713 2009
  843'.914—dc22   2009006985

CONTENTS

ABOVE ALL, DON'T LOOK BACK

AUTHOR'S NOTE

This is a novel. The setting in which I have placed my characters was to a great extent inspired by the region where an earthquake struck, on May 21, 2003, shaking much of northern Algeria and causing immense material and human loss. It should not, however, be considered a reconstitution. The entirely fictitious characters inhabiting these places could bear a resemblance to existing or previously existing people. This is one of the probabilities inherent in the nature of the project.

M. B.

This text is dedicated to those women and men whose lives were lost or turned upside down on a day in Algeria, in the year 2003. It is also dedicated to the countless victims of the tsunami that hit Asia on December 26, 2004, and whose shock wave shook us all.

Epigraph- phrase, quotation or poem set @ the beginning of a document/book. It serves as a preface, summary, counter-example or to link the work to a wider literary base, either to invite comparison or to enlist a conventional context

Universalizes trauma
- Bey makes it so that anyone can read and appreciate this book, anyone who has gone through something similar.

Bey covers herself, she didn't want to cause controversy or upset so she says it's not real. Universalizes trauma. What the author says in the first two ¶, influences how we read the rest of the novel.

To Isma, ma mou

I is someone else.
—Arthur Rimbaud

Thing of mystery, Me, are you living yet!
When dawn's curtain lifts, you will recognize
Your same bitter self . . .
Farewell, thought I, mortal Me, sister, falsehood.
—Paul Valéry, *La jeune Parque* (trans. David Paul)

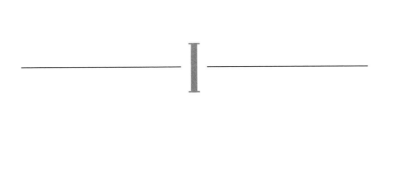

I

I walk through the streets of the city.

I walk forward, behind or ahead of—I don't know, I'm not sure, but what does it matter—ahead of or behind a dense cloud of intermingled dust and ashes.

I cut across streets, avenues, boulevards, cul-de-sacs, passageways, alleys—now only paths through heaps of stone, earth.

And this outrageously swollen instant has become a shrill noise, a naked space swallowing time.

Trees as sentinels, ineffectually guarding their posts.

I walk on, disappearing into the defeated city—distorted, destroyed, dispersed.

I walk on and everything in front of me abruptly cuts off my breath, my gaze—penetrates my flesh.

Sharp pain, sharper, fiercer that a woman's scream, seems to gush out of the earth itself. It overflows the banks of each wound, empties itself, hollows out its bed, gets lost among the ruins, dwindles, returns, more virulent than ever, as if revived by having reached the very core of its being, then rises to the bizarre tan, yellowish sky before dissolving into the clouds.

I walk on through the streets of the city.

I look all around me. Eyelids hurting from trying to keep my eyes open. Wide open.

I am walking.

The odor is there, at first faint, like a hazy ring of light. An odor exuding from this enormous cesspool—with its guts open, exposed to the air. I catch whiffs of it like the ones that surface when you poke the green, stagnant water of a swamp with a stick. Musty emanations from deep underground. With nightfall, the odor spreads. It's with me wherever I go. It slinks along the ground. It slips first into the folds of my dress. Then it slides along my legs, climbing up, slowly slithering. It gets into my mouth, my nostrils, drips through my hair. Millimeter by millimeter—it coats me, encrusts me. It leaves stains of smoke and shadow all along my hands. On my skin, my entire body.

It's inside me. It is now my companion. I in turn have been infected. But I'm still alive.

People step aside as I walk by.

It's all I am now, all I'll ever be. I'll no longer be the girl I was. I'll be nothing more than the odor assimilated that day. A bitter offensive stench of dust, rot, and decaying carcasses.

I walk on for a long time. An infinitely long time—beyond all dimensions, beyond all spans of time.

The evening comes to meet me.

I sit down. Surprised by the night, I grow faint. My head back, I search in vain for stars.

Darkness gradually penetrates me. The water of the night slowly rises. I am drowned by it. Let myself flow.

Then it's day.

Now light is reborn and gray dawn spreads itself over the world tasting of earth and ashes.

What? Time wasn't swallowed up by the earth then? I don't understand. How is it possible that the world hasn't stopped turning in order to contemplate its work?

An entire lifetime wouldn't be enough time to tell what I've seen. What I am seeing.

Speak up or remain silent forever.

Sometimes I have to stop. When there's nothing to look at. I've come too far. It's all scrub over there. Brambles. I turn back. Keep my eyes open.

Over there, children are playing. No, they're not playing; they're slipping in and out of crevasses. Searching, no doubt, for some precious or useless object—I don't know, I'm not sure, but what does it matter? Nimble and full of life, they call out to each other and jump over mountains of rubble.

A woman is leaning back—straight, rigid—as if holding herself up against an expanse of ruined wall. Or else trying to hold it up. A wall that's all white. She has a black bag in one hand, a red bundle in the other. She doesn't move an inch when I walk past her. She isn't looking at me. Eyes empty. Absent.

No one is talking. And yet it's not silent.
No one is talking to me.
No one is looking at me.
Over there, set off against the livid sky, a row of electric poles are curiously bent over, all in the same direction, with their lines ripped off.

At the top of a pile of debris, there are two young men with bare chests. They lean over. They straighten up again. You'd say they were praying. They're removing stones and debris. They're gathering bits of wood, pieces of glass, scraps of metal. They toss them back over their shoulders. Same gesture. Same cadence. They lean over. They straighten up. A strange prayer. Below, all around, men urge them on with their voices.

Farther off stand other men. Lined up at their feet lie figures stretched out. Bodies covered in white shrouds or brightly colored blankets. Soft. Plush. At this moment, who wouldn't like to be all warm under a blanket? *Earthquake = metaphor for the hard times Algeria had as a country.*

I am walking. *They were under French conquest, then had*
Sunshine.
Thirst. *a war for independence, & then a civil war*
Incandescence. *occurred, Algeria has cracked/shattered/fallen*
Hunger. *much like the aftermath of an earthquake*
From time to time, the ground gives way under my feet. A tremor. Another. And still another. Everything freezes.

That blue line, so reassuring in its absolute horizontality, in the distance, the far distance, might just be the sea. Farther off, it is the sea. Rocks submerged for centuries break the surface now, only a few meters from the beach. Not very far away.

Hundreds of birds have taken refuge in precarious shelters all along the shore. Dried shrubs, heaps of incandescent stones, hollow trees in human shapes, as if struck by lightning, lying here and there. You only notice the living presence of the crazed

ABOVE ALL, DON'T LOOK BACK

birds by the imperceptible rubbing of their wings over the sand. A light, regular rustling like an echo of the slow, ever so slow, waves pounding the shore today. From time to time the dry crackling of stones heated white-hot by the sun—motionless for long hours—in the center of the white sky. Blinding light, violent reverberation, a heaviness weighing on everything, and, above all, silence, the interminable, intolerable vibration of silence.

I stop. I can't go any further. I can't keep on. My body, my legs refuse me.

Nearby, over there—yes, there—the wailing of sirens. But for whom are those snakes that . . .

The flies are voracious. More and more numerous. More and more aggressive. Swarms of flies blacken the edge of the city. They block out the light. They cover the screen. Their buzzing grows louder. Swelling. Swelling. Drones in the ears. Flashes of lightning cross the horizon. They are coming closer. They bristle against me. Burn me.

Thirst.

Pain.

I am lying in the dust. Weakened and drooping in turn. Minuscule, pathetic, stubborn, I try to keep going. I creep. I try. Knees, elbows, hands clawing at the dust.

The horizon is blocked by metal beams and concrete blocks with razor-sharp edges. All I can see when I look around me are gaping wounds, great abysses.

Amid the rubble: rags make blotches of color like spots of blood. Scraps of fabric attached to rusty, twisted branches clacking in the wind. A sign wobbles back and forth. A slow, repetitive motion marked by a faint creaking noise. To the right. Then left. Right. Left. How I would like to decipher those words! I draw closer. Very close. CONSTRUCTION MATERIAL. I can. I can still read.

ABOVE ALL, DON'T LOOK BACK

Emerging from the very center of the earth, a fragment of fused light breaks free. It comes to fix itself inside me. Slices right through me. From one side to the other. A horrendous clamor erupts from the depths of my being. It bounces back and forth, echoing, nearby at first, deafening, then, little by little, growing distant, and more distant, smothered in silence. It comes back to me. Engulfs me. Sucks me toward a bottomless pit. An utterly white void. Utterly black. I don't know. I'm not sure.

Without any resistance, I let myself be borne along in a whirlwind of sand and ashes.

Abyss.

Incandescence.

Darkness.

It seems that I screamed once, only once, just before opening my eyes. I have no recollection.

I have always found the following expression very useful and very intriguing: "for reasons beyond our control." For while it may be structured like a causal circumstantial clause, it actually tells you the exact opposite of what you expect, giving you no explanation at all, even though its whole purpose is supposed to be to explain, to justify incidents and unforeseen, often aggravating complications. And above all, because it opens the way for all kinds of hypotheses.

I could hide behind that and start off with the welcome expression that would place this whole story under the sign of contingency or lack of responsibility right from the beginning. However, I have to tell you straight off that I don't believe in mere chance. Whether it be singular or plural.

I don't believe in coincidence either.

I believe that everything is a sign. A bit as if we—fragile, fallible, and yet supposedly reasonable creatures—were caught inside an invisible web. A web woven by the facts in order to reach a finality that seems imperceptible, incomprehensible at first. And even if the original causes of each event are obscure in the beginning, they very quickly become discernible, as long as you go to the trouble of considering the unfolding of events, and above all the way they link up together.

I very sincerely believe that everything happening to each and every one of us follows a kind of logic, perhaps even a will, that is inside us but of which we are unaware. I am not talking about fate or divine intervention. I'll leave that to others. To you perhaps, about whom I know nothing, and who are there just to listen to me. To those who want to pull all the strings today and crush us under the weight of their certainties. To those who control the keys for explaining the world and opening the gates of paradise. To the numerous, ever-increasing number of those who, assisted by powerful proclamations of fatwa, are perfectly able to adapt speeches and dictates opportunistically to their own needs under the guise of moral and religious precepts. And to those who, in the same spirit, believe themselves invested with the power to prohibit or to permit, to make pronouncements, and to approve eruditely or else to reject the sayings and doings of those men and women who are not exactly like them.

This opening section—perhaps a bit too long, perhaps a bit too argumentative—had one purpose only: to help me find a beginning to this story. To get you conditioned, you who are listening to me and trying to understand. Maybe it is an explanation also, a justification for all the actions reported with precision in the narration that follows. As a result I won't need to go very far back in time, back into my childhood and the numerous snags that have caught at the surface or else plunged deeply into the course of my life.

Introduce, because you have to begin with the beginning, or so they have told me. Introduce the facts with the following sentence, the following statement, acting as if people really believe it: if my life was turned upside down in one single day, it is due to the conjunction of two natural phenomena, that is to say, phenomena exterior to myself and, most importantly, independent of all human will.

First of all, a climatic anomaly. It was a summer day without golden hues and light. A summer day the color of sand and storm. Everything was unclear, blurry, blanketed in an unbreathable, heavy atmosphere. One of those whims that the hot seasons have had in store for us these last years, ever since the desert began advancing without remission.

Allow me to specify: a very low sky, marked by thick reddish clouds. Billions of particles floating in the air. Throat: harsh, parched. Furtive crunching under footsteps. Layers of red dust along the surface of the ground.

This induces a strange fever. A sort of overall itchiness that will end up spreading and increasing in intensity the more you try to apply words to the accompanying symptoms. This can even lead to the most unexpected of physical signs: clenched fists and jaw, uncontrollable shaking, impatience, and excessive weakness. As if under the effect of a muted anger born before its exact origin could be found. The kind of anger that skews all judgment. And can, when it bursts, devastate an entire life. Yes, that could be it. Everything points to the fact that there exists, in each one of us, an underground river whose source seems to be in the murmurs of the first mornings, in the first gaze laid upon us, in the tempests and torments of childhood, in the millions of threads ceaselessly woven and sometimes broken, in the too smooth passage of days and the overwhelming gentleness of long summer nights. A river that is sometimes serene, sometimes violent. And sometimes it happens that the course of this river gets blocked. Dammed up. Too forcefully. For too long. So it builds up an uncontrollable force, searches for the slightest breach to burst through and flow forth freely.

First of all then, a gust blown in from the South. A powerful, harmful wind that sweeps away everything not firmly attached to the ground.

Then, at a few minutes to eight in the evening, another event, of an entirely different intensity. A totally unpredictable event, with devastating consequences for its part: an earthquake.

A sudden feeling of vertigo. Preceded by a muted rumble, similar to a distant drum roll or the furious surge of an endless herd that has been locked in the depths of the very earth. The ground gives away. Dizziness as the light fixtures start trembling. There is only time to realize that yes, it is the earth, the earth that has shaken, that is still shaking.

But the realization comes very quickly.

And everyone starts screaming all at once. We stand up. We start running.

Running every which way. Without thinking anything other than get out, get away, run away, as fast as possible, as far as possible. Everyone for himself. And the earth—for a moment still, stationary, gathering its force, only to begin shaking again, like some monstrous beast—rocks once again. A second time. As if to shake off or get rid of the burden of a humanity become too weighty.

ABOVE ALL, DON'T LOOK BACK

Get out.
Get away.
Run away.
As far as possible.
As fast as possible.

And the earth—for a moment still, stationary, gathering its force, only to begin shaking again, like some monstrous beast—rocks once again. A second time. As if to shake off or get rid of the burden of a humanity become too weighty.

We scream.

We try to get out. We look for exits. All of us at once. We shove each other. Stumble. Trample each other underfoot. We fall. Stand back up again. Complain. And everyone invokes their mother first, of course—*yemma, yemma lahbiba*—most beloved mother, dead or alive, first sanctuary as in the early days of childhood. And we forget to be civil, or even to be humane. Only the blind instinct for self-preservation remains . . . Veneers crack.

Once the shock wave has passed, we call out to each other: did anyone, anyone, think of the documents, the money, the jewelry, the keys? We approach the front door hesitantly, taking our time to make sure everything is still standing. That the walls are still upright. That it's okay, it's okay now, the worst has surely passed . . . We consult each other over the possibility of a third aftershock before taking the chance of returning to the house to recover essentials: documents, money, jewelry—yes, there, in the safe . . . and then . . . everything is calm again. An uneasy calm, heavy with a form of anxiety that won't lift for a long time. Eventually we go inside. But we don't close the doors. Not right away. Then we check to make sure everything has stayed in place. We examine the room. List the material damage, inconsequential, thanks be to God. Some cracks in the ceiling, a few fissures in the wall, a few shattered glasses in the dining-room sideboard and a fallen picture of father, framed and enlarged, showing him next to the president of the Republic, who had come to inaugurate the construction zone for a new subsidized housing project. Nothing major.

The inevitable comments ensue concerning the frailty of man in the face of the relentless force of the elements and of divine will. Always punctuated, of course, by invocations to God aimed at keeping at bay any harmful events that could affect the physical and mental integrity of The Family.

Then all the commotion subsides. Everything snaps back into place. Just as quickly. We gather around the table for dinner.

Of course, it's obvious. It would take a lot more than a mild tremor to shake up their assured sense of invulnerability.

Yes, it takes a lot more to shake up a life. To hurl a life into the night, like pebbles at the pit of a well.

I recall that before falling asleep, in that hazy phase of drifting off that heralds dreams, I thought: tomorrow my mother will be up early. Even earlier than usual. On days after sandstorms she is like a bee, frazzled by the urgency and extent of the tasks that await her, or more precisely the tasks that just can't wait. A little more nervous than usual, if that is possible. She flits about here and there, she whirls—or more accurately considering how small and light she is—spins like a top, her skirts and imprecations swirling about her. Terribly diligent, terribly efficient. It would make anybody dizzy who tried to keep up. And Dalila, our old housekeeper who now comes to help twice a week, will no doubt have to work many hours of overtime. Compensated, as usual, by a few leftover scraps from supper, plus a downpour of blessings, which are, as everybody knows, worth so much more than any other form of payment. They might even call her niece Amina in for reinforcement. The house is very big after all.

From the cellar to the terrace, everything will be scrutinized by the inquiring eyes of the Supreme Official before being moved, scrubbed down ruthlessly, polished, vacuumed, scoured, and sanitized by the surefire action of bleach, scented cresol, and other disinfectants. My mother is an emeritus housekeeper, cited several times by the OMH, the Order of Meticulous Housekeepers. Praise be to Housekeeping, that god so demanding before whom she prostrates herself each day. Tomorrow, watch out anyone who tries to get in her way. But tomorrow, I thought, tomorrow I'll be far away.

That's all.

I must have fallen asleep very quickly. With just this sentence in my head. Like a prayer to the night, or an epitaph really: may the winds blow and sweep away my footprints.

Yes, I must have fallen asleep very quickly. I must have dreamed as well. I awoke with the odor still encrusted in every corner of the room, in every crease of my dress. Or maybe it was the odor itself that woke me. I don't know. I'm not sure. I think it was the day after that I left. Yes, I think that is right.

ABOVE ALL, DON'T LOOK BACK

At the bottom of the stairs I stopped to look at myself one last time in the large mirror that hangs over the dresser near the doorway. Then I crossed the threshold and gently pulled the door closed behind me.

At least I think so.

Here, at present, is a step-by-step, hour-by-hour reconstitution of the various stages of my journey. The most essential ones. Right up to this day which brings me toward you.

It is the hour of prayer. Despite the insistent calls of muezzins flooding out from loudspeakers turned up high, the streets and environs of the mosques remain desperately vacant. Scattered here and there, barely a small handful of believers more daring than the others. Shadows hug the walls before plunging hastily into the House of God. For more than a week now, a heat wave, in combination with the sandstorm, has imposed a curfew well before the hour.

In the heart of summer, in this village, and in this entire country crushed by the heat and the sun, there is a feeling of torpor close to a trance that takes hold of all beings after a certain time of the day.

I walk through the empty streets, silently savoring my state of very precarious elation in not being seen, recognized, and tracked down.

Off in the distance, a hollow rumble seems to signal a coming storm. We have already been waiting for days. It approaches the town—just barely brushes it—skirts around and moves off, as if discouraged by a couple of mediocre performances. It trails away, not even bothering to burst into shower, like all summer thunderstorms. No need to look up and examine the sky. Even the most discriminating meteorologist wouldn't be able to find a single rain-bearing cloud.

I have always heard it said by those around me that you would have to be crazy to go out at this time of day. One of those numerous affirmations that end up bearing the full weight of truth. For how many poor souls, so they say, have been carried home feverish with froth dripping from their mouths, their bodies thrashing about in violent convulsions, after having been *struck* by the sun!

Yes, that must be it. I am a bit crazy, there is no doubt about it. Just a touch or hint of insanity . . . Otherwise, I wouldn't have come to this place, at this hour, and on this day. I wouldn't have left my house without the slightest intention of turning back.

And I certainly wouldn't be here telling you my story, trying to find an order, a chronology, some kind of logic to my acts.

In our country, it is important to realize that a woman is already considered to be crazy—or to stay more within the accepted range of expressions, mentally disturbed—when, for example, she leaves her home in a sudden irrational impulse without having said or asked anything of anyone. There are also those who gravitate naturally toward others. Without ulterior motives, apprehension, or bad intention. Those who speak up. Who go out without a veil. Who express themselves openly. Who develop a friendship, or, being all excess and immoderation, a full-fledged passion for all that moves and creates motion: the clouds overhead, music, rain, light, wind, the sun and stars in the sky, the leaves in the trees, and the tiny creatures sheltered therein. Those who, impudently, look you straight in the eye and say no. And in this way say: I want it or I don't want it. I'll do it or I won't do it. I'll go or I won't go. Those who—not caring about staring eyes and the stir created when they simply walk by—go as far as opening up, ready to confront criticism and judgment without the slightest trace of the modesty that makes a woman lower her eyes and blush delicately. Those women who let their laughter ring out with deliberate insolence in front of whoever happens to be listening. Who scoff at all respectability, discretion, reserve and propriety, appearances-that-must-be-kept-up-at-all-costs. And finally, those who simply, discreetly or brazenly—despite it all and in spite of everyone—throw off all their chains. Those who, in the process of breaking their shackles, end up leaving, finally liberated, finally free.

Crazy? Until now, I was crazy, but only to a degree that was more or less acceptable. Within fluctuating limits that were more or less tolerable. For insanity, as we know, depends on the norms laid down by a society—that model of cohesion, coherence, and everlasting harmony, without the slightest trace of dissonance. I would be more like a discordant note, nothing more. Kind of like that screeching sound that chalk makes across a blackboard every now and then. Bad quality chalk at that, just like everything made in this country, as my exasperated Arabic teacher put it one day, before pitching the object of his rage at the head of the pupil who was seated nearest to him.

The shrillness of a noise that aggravates, that disturbs. Worse still, that exasperates.

I quite like the comparison.

At present, I must retrace every last detail of this journey.
A journey at the end of which I thought I would find myself
again, find what I'd forgotten. The first thing, or the last. I
don't know. I'm not sure.

It will be like a writing assignment with the following in-
structions: tell what you saw, did, and heard. Don't forget to
describe the impressions that you had along the way.

The florid face of the bus driver is sporting a thick mustache. At the end of his strong hairy arms, his surprisingly
small, almost atrophied hands grip the wheel firmly. His pull-
over of a questionable shade of white has large sweat stains
looping under his arms and down along his back.

Of course, he recognizes me right away. He lives in my
neighborhood. I have crossed paths with him before. Even if he
doesn't know my first name, he knows who I am.

It seems that I can read him, as if there were a parchment
gradually unrolling as he watches me come up the steps. Yes
indeed, that young woman who just got on the bus is definitely
the daughter of Hajj Abderrahmane, the richest entrepreneur
in town. Yes indeed—he leans over, studies, scrutinizes—that's
the oldest girl all right, the one who works as a monitor at the
local high school. Even though it took a fair amount of dealing
apparently, it's been official for a long time now: she is the fi-
ancée of the son of Si M'Hamed, the tax collector. An excellent
alliance.

And as far as he's concerned, he can look forward to major feasts in the near future. Because in The Family, things are
never done by halves. My father is planning on inviting our entire neighborhood to the wedding festivities, which are scheduled to last three days and three nights. It's the first child he
has married off, and his reputation is very important to him.
What's more, the elections are approaching. He must show the
full extent of his generosity. And if it is God's will, and his
schemes bear fruit, in good time El Hajj will attain one of his
goals. He will become a member of parliament. The marriage is

set for two weeks before the legislative elections. In exactly one month and fifteen days.

Ah, but if he only knew! If they all just realized that it takes but a few words, but a few seconds, to shatter time and all forms of certainty, to wreck all your plans and snap all the strings. And that afterward, it is difficult to weave everything together again, to recover . . . to reassemble all the bits of scattered time that are sharper than shards of glass.

I greet the man who will help me accomplish the first stage of this journey, at the end of which I will perhaps find myself again, perhaps find what I've forgotten. I utter a very polite phrase and smile widely. He is taken aback. A young girl traveling alone inevitably arouses strong suspicion.

"You're alone?" he asks.

"Yes, Ammi Mohammed."

I call him Ammi Mohammed without having to worry about getting it wrong. We call all men of our father's age "uncle," a polite expression that is meant to establish mutual respect, and for that generation, in nearly all families, the oldest child was quite naturally named after the Prophet.

I try to act naturally. This implies: lowered gaze, awkward gestures. It has to be made blaringly obvious: I am intimidated, almost frightened, which is what one expects from a girl of a good family, unaccustomed to being out alone.

"And where do you plan on going like that?"

"To my aunt's house in Algiers."

To slip through the net hanging over every house in this village simply cannot be done. We're just one big happy family. Close-knit and watchful over everything. Particularly over people's joys and sorrows. With a clear preference for the tragedies, for, as everyone knows, these allow a person the indefeasible right to exercise compassion. And in this way one can multiply one's number of Good Deeds, which are calculated according to a strictly codified system, G.D. that bring automatic access to paradise. At least this is the widely accepted view, held by the majority of the population.

We are just one big happy family. With the same hatreds. The same jealousy. The same malice carefully dissimulated behind façades that are all the more polished from one person to the next, and behind heaps of standard polite phrases passed down from our ancestors. Consecrated phrases, which have taken on the patina and uselessness of junk acquired through inheritance. Phrases completely devoid of sense, like the ones I too can recite, one after another, counting them off like prayer beads whenever I happen to bump into someone I know on the village roads.

Along the way I have thought up all the replies, the lies that must remove any suspicion. The phrases are linked one after another in my head with such ease and simplicity that it even surprises me. Thus, to completely convince the driver, who is a bit intrigued, I have all the explanations ready to roll off my tongue. I make the first move.

"My aunt's so tired these days. She's been working a lot lately. El Hajj wants me to go visit her and give her a hand. She needs me. He was here with me earlier, but he couldn't stay to wait. He had to get back to the construction zone. You know how he is, always working so much! And the workers . . . well, with this heat and all . . . He told me to pass along his greetings, and he asks you to watch over me."

By these measured words, said with just the right dose of suavity in my voice, respect in my gaze, and friendliness in my words, the good man is clearly convinced. Here is an example of a girl raised to respect traditions. May grace be upon mothers and fathers of merit! My completely believable explanation has reassured him in his role as guardian in the absence of a family member. He looks all around him as if making the other passengers—who are overwhelmed by the suffocating closeness inside the vehicle and the stench of iron and sweat circulating impudently about—witnesses to his sudden promotion. He puffs right up. With a benevolent gesture, he points to the seat directly behind him. This way he can keep an eye on me by glancing in his rearview mirror from time to time.

All the seat cushions have deep slashes in them. Metal springs poke out, finally freed of all restraint. Before sitting down, I place a plastic bag on the seat. It contains a few rags I have hastily stuffed inside so I am not traveling empty-handed, and this gives plausibility to my story. I'll have to be careful when I stand back up again. My skirt might catch on the end of a spring, as if it were a fishhook. And I don't have anything else to wear.

He inquires:

"Do you know exactly where she lives?"

"Yes, near the Place du Cheval, in the city center. But don't worry about me, someone will be there waiting for me at the bus stop. Either my cousin or my uncle. We phoned them."

He nods. He is taking his role seriously. Everything seems to be under control, for the time being anyway. I am several hours ahead of Them.

To avoid being thoroughly interrogated in front of the other passengers, I can't risk giving him time for any more questions. I launch into conversation. With a lure that should work right away.

"Oh this heat! It's unbearable! It must be really hard for you, driving back and forth in your bus all day long! Tell me, Ammi Mohammed, is it this hot in Algiers?"

It's a method tested in hammams, waiting rooms, beauty salons, buses, and shared taxis: nothing better to facilitate conversation than diving headlong into the vast topic of unusual weather occurrences. And it works like a charm every time. A fascinating topic on which everyone has something to say, and all opinions can be shared without things getting out of hand. At least when you don't venture onto shifting ground.

He gets going right away. Yes, of course, this heat. Summertime. Dryness, a sure sign of God's exasperation in the face of the indescribable arrogance of his creatures. All the passengers get in their two cents' worth as the driver steers onto the highway to leave the city. General discussion ensues. Shaken out of their apathy by the urgent need to express themselves, the passengers—only the men, of course, that goes without saying—inaugurate a remarkably elaborate, eclectic debate. And, in veneration of a recently acquired right, namely the freedom of speech, every topic gets treated. Blowing sand. The constant advance of the desert. The negligence of authorities in all institutions. The lack of hygiene. The housing crisis and subsequent upheavals due to the distribution of subsidized units, which is always done unfairly. Rockets, satellites, and satellite dishes. Violence breaking out in stadiums. Corruption. Pollution. The misappropriation of public funds. Nepotism. The contraband problem. The exchange rate for the euro. American hegemony. CNN. Al Jazeera. Iraq. Palestine. Terrorism. Staged roadblocks. The true-false mujahideen. And then, finally, the very recent earthquake, whose damage and death toll have had little effect on this lovely region, well removed from the epicenter. Fair enough, in light of all that has just been said. A disagreement flares up on the magnitude and number of victims declared by the officials that very morning, which brings them back to the negligence of the authorities and their refined craft of dissimulation. This provides everyone with an opportunity to utter the standard phrase called for under such circumstances, inserted between a pair of virulent and definitive condemnations: God protect us from the evils that are engendered by the pride of those who are deaf and blind to His warnings. *Amen.*

The journey continues. I continue. For you. The retorts are all merging together. The words interweaving above my head. The phrases mixing together. Swarms of words are attacking my tired conscience. I hurt all over. I have a headache. A droning in my ears. Moments of vertigo. Landscapes. Faces. Everything is spinning. Everything is getting mixed up. I move on. I leave . . .

My head resting against the hot glass, I pretend to doze off. I don't feel like meeting the concerned eyes of my provisional protector, who gazes at me every now and then.

ABOVE ALL, DON'T LOOK BACK

At the next village, an elderly woman enveloped in an old-fashioned white haik boards the bus and comes to sit next to me. She clings to my arm before allowing herself to plop down on the seat. No doubt exhausted from the heat plus the effort of climbing the bus's three steps, she is having trouble catching her breath. A few moments later, she begins to dig around in her bag. She nearly empties out its entire contents before pulling out a bottle of water, which is wrapped in a damp rag meant to keep it cool. She opens the bottle, brings it to her mouth, and sips the water with a repulsive, almost obscene sucking noise before holding the bottle out to me without a word. She is staring at me. She is talking to me. I think. Her lips are moving. I can see them. But I don't hear her. A puff of air. A hissing at my ears. Her eyes are pale, as though partially faded. In the corner of her lips, a string of saliva drips down, getting lost in the meandering curves of a deep wrinkle before reaching the very tip of her chin, drooping, hesitating in midair, and then splattering on her knees. I don't dare refuse the water she offers me. I drink one mouthful only. The water is lukewarm and stale. I'm not thirsty. I'm not hungry. I no longer have any recollection of my last meal. There is a rumbling in my stomach, but I don't feel any sensation of emptiness. At noon, with my stomach in a knot, I couldn't swallow a thing. Nobody noticed. For a long time now, I've been completely free, in that domain at least. We live together, as a family, which doesn't necessarily mean that we pay attention to one another. For the Family is nothing but a closely woven community, which must be made to appear unified in everyone's eyes, for better and for worse. A community of individual interests, which must be made to coincide in order to achieve a common objective: the preservation of material wealth and the honor attached to the family name. That's all.

Just before I arrive at my destination, I can't help but glance back. One last time. I must, so that you will understand, so that you will have all the elements in hand. I am thus going to stage the play that will be acted out in my wake.

I have always known how to invent scenes, situations. In order to keep control. Because that is what it is all about. You must, you must stay in control.

I know the characters so well that there is no way I will get the casting wrong, nor the various reactions brought on by The Disappearance.

Now I hear the distinct sound of voices calling out. More and more insistently. Interspersed with endless commentary. Ah, that girl, the day will come when we'll have to outright forbid her from locking herself in her room all day long to read or get out of housework! She's over twenty years old and continues to act like an irresponsible little girl! She has always been so odd and unpredictable. But this is too much, on the night before her own wedding! You wonder how! But that will change, and she will have no choice but to . . . How I wish she would go, just go live somewhere else!

Then, shortly after that the screaming would begin. The threats. The bewilderment in the face of silence. The empty bedroom. The slamming doors. There would be a lot of noise and a lot of fury. Questions. The questioning of the two sisters. Presumed accomplices.

Next, as is easily understood, would come the time of utter astonishment. Nobody, nobody at all, could have imagined that one day I would actually find within myself the audacity necessary to leave the house without having told someone, without having asked for permission first. She dared leave! It's not even possible! Unthinkable! She really has it coming to her!

They would wait for several hours in any case. Two or more. Enough time to sharpen their weapons and put their sanctions in place. Then, gradually, an increasing feeling of panic would hone itself on the razor-sharp edge of the time spent waiting. An uncontrollable feeling of anxiety. And not just over me, need-less to say. There would be the most terrible, the most formi-dable of ordeals to think about: what-people-are-going-to-say. Relatives. Close and distant. Numerous friends of the Fam-ily. Acquaintances. Neighbors—in particular the women. Ex-future in-laws. My father's clients and his workers. Members of the party. Future voters. My brother's friends. Passersby. Men sitting on the terraces of the cafés. Youth leaning up against the walls. The police. The gendarmes. Military men. The city's authorities. Peddlers. Masseurs at the hammam. Those look-ing out from behind their blinds. The tongues of vipers. Those who are concerned. Those who are indifferent. Everyone. Ev-ery single one of them. Everyone who always has something to say about everything.

They would consult together before calling our neighbor, Yemma Khadija, to find out if I happened to be there. Without sounding too insistent. She has been living alone since her two sons were killed by terrorists in a false roadblock. Sometimes I went over to her house to keep her company, but never without having first informed those who safeguard the honor of The Family day and night.

Then they would close the doors again. The windows too. You never know.

They would look in my room. They would open the closet to see if I had taken my purse, my bag, my suitcase, or some of my personal belongings. They would inventory all the objects left behind without regret. Surveying it all in painstaking de-tail.

In an attempt to be reassuring perhaps, someone would say: she left everything behind. Everything. Nothing is miss-ing. Not even her underwear. She didn't take a thing with her. Not her jewelry, not her identification documents, not even her fiancé's gifts. Would they perhaps consider flipping through or reading my notebooks for clues? Would they decide to call my future mother-in-law to ask how their future son-in-law was doing, and to talk about the wedding preparations? Just to see if . . . You never know . . . And along the same lines, I think that they would try to check with Mériem, the dressmaker, who was in the process of making me evening gowns and caftans that were even more superbly embroidered than the trousseaux already prepared for other girls in the village, as my mother insisted should be the case. Or else they would try to get information from her daughter Leila, who happened to be a student at the lycée where I worked.

Someone would say: well she won't be able to go very far without any money or anything.

So the time would come to search every last corner of the house. Every single room, one at a time, leaving nothing to chance. They would remember my love of games and secret little places. They would look under beds. Under tables. In cupboards. Under the stairs. Then on the terrace. They would inconspicuously inspect the surroundings of the house. Finally, they would meet together to discuss what to do. There would be my father, urgently summoned, all sweating and out of breath. My mother. And my two sisters too. They would remain standing with their arms entwined—inseparable twins—as one. Perhaps even my brother would be summoned, provided they managed to find him, provided he was finished taking drags from his joint.

True to character, he would come straight to the point.

He would say, his mouth all twisted with rage and fury, with a form of hatred come from much further back than this day alone: "She's crazy, crazy, completely insane . . . she's a tramp . . . she's a . . . I already warned you!"

And perhaps he wouldn't dare utter the unutterable word that would come to his lips first. Not in front of his mother and father. He still has a few remnants of respect left toward them, at least in language matters. But he would find a way to clearly suggest it anyway. He would storm out of the room and slam the door shut. Even making the walls quake. And he would play his part right to the end. He would comb through the streets of the neighborhood. He would search even the most inconsequential alleyways and cul-de-sacs of the village. The gardens. The cemetery where the twins and I would go to play when we were little. All of this done without asking anyone anything. Absolutely not! As if nothing were wrong. With the fear of scandal knotted in his stomach, more painful than a bout of renal colic. *Kechfa!** This is precisely what gives me a head start. My precious advantage over them! And, because of serious and long-term family disputes, they wouldn't be able to question anyone. They wouldn't even talk about it with my aunt in Algiers. Especially not her! She would be too pleased. Ever since she started trying to pry into our affairs.

And once all the turbulence subsides, they would say: well anyway . . . we already knew.

A complete about-face, considering the serious and urgent nature of the situation.

Yes, I've always known. All those periods of silence, all those averted gazes . . . How did I manage to live so long with this thing oppressing me?

Later, in the evening, the doors locked and the slatted shutters snapped shut once again, they would unearth the family chronicles. They would cite words. Phrases. They would reexamine certain behavior, attitudes, and conduct. They would go back in time. And then they would have to prepare themselves for the questions. Quickly come up with various alternative scenarios. First, a temporary one to ward off the more insistent curiosity seekers. A story at once believable and convincing. They would need a cover. They would have to build, cut, assemble, patch together, embroider. Find the most sensible and prudent justification for this disaster, this unforeseen catastrophe: the disappearance of a girl the day after an earthquake. For reasons still unknown. A story that could be modified if necessary at a later time according to unfolding events. And in the Family, no one is a novice. Everyone's suggestions would be considered. Should they alert my father's numerous contacts to get a search underway? Yes, but how to explain it? How to

---

*A scandal giving rise to shame for the whole family. —TRANS.

present the thing? No! Not right away. For now, they would have to put up a front. The whole thing had to be thought through before making a decision. We all had to be united in our misfortune. And we weren't going to let ourselves be confounded by lies. By insidious allusions. Deadly little phrases. By assaults of questions that wouldn't fail to hit their mark.

The first attack would come very quickly. And without a doubt from the family's closest friend, Yamina, otherwise known as The Weasel. A perfect match for my mother, nicknamed by all the neighborhood girls El Khabar, after the country's most widely read daily newspaper. Both of them, with piercing gazes and quivering nostrils, were perpetually on the prowl for the nauseating stench of scandal, for a few good rumors to dig up. These, they felt, could carry the flow of resentment seething inside, aggravating the encrusted bitterness that had been maintained for so long, letting all feelings of generosity atrophy and impregnating everything coming out of their mouths with venom; yet they were never soothed in the slightest and the void in their existence remained unfilled.

She would say, with the gentle worried expression of someone genuinely concerned about the well-being of those dearest: "By the way, how is your daughter Amina? We haven't seen her in such a long time!"

Or else: "And what about Amina? Hasn't she come home yet? We miss seeing that dear girl! Did she go out to finish shopping for her trousseau?"

Or finally, to drive the nail in: "How are the wedding preparations coming along? Do you need any help? Don't forget, my dear, I'm always here if you need me."

At present, before my eyes, I can very clearly see my mother's face fraught with defeat. Her gradual breakdown. Hour by hour. Her muttering. Her imprecations. Her curses. "May God curse the day you were conceived and the womb that carried you" is one of her favorites. It is reserved exclusively for me. It resonates in my ears so often that I can hear it distinctly, even when she is just looking at me in silence.

ABOVE ALL, DON'T LOOK BACK

She comes and goes, moving from one room to another. As she walks, she presses her temples with both hands. In the hallway, she suddenly stops. As far as she can see, there is only one possible reason for my departure: The Fault. But where? When? How? And most importantly, most importantly, with whom? She knows how uninterested and even repulsed I am by Ali, the man the Family has officially dubbed my suitor. So, how can it be explained? Is it possible that the girl would have let herself be taken advantage of? Her? No, impossible! And it's simply unfathomable that she wouldn't have seen or noticed anything, when every single month, since the very first time, she has marked down the precise dates of the girls' periods on a calendar hanging on the fridge in the kitchen: a green triangle for Mouna and a blue circle for Fatima.

She begins pacing once again. She stops short. Again. She rocks back and forth on her feet. She holds her belly, as though overwhelmed by contractions. Then she straightens up again. In passing, she notes the dust accumulated on the windowsill. Wipes it off with the tips of her fingers. Sighs. She didn't have time to finish cleaning house. She searches for someone she can lay her anger on. It has been a long time since they let go of Dalila, housekeeper and silent witness to family turmoil. They had known her for a long time and knew she wouldn't talk, but it was better to be cautious. My mother looks around her. She notices her two daughters slouched at the bottom of the stairwell and scolds them as she goes by. Her hands nervously finger the corner of her apron or the end of her belt.

I imagine Mouna and Fatima's unfeigned worry. They don't know anything. They wring their hands. In an identical gesture. They don't dare cry. Exchange looks of desperation. Swear, in identical shaking voices, that they saw nothing, heard nothing. But they would take the time to interrogate them all the same. To threaten them. To punish them. And then, after that, to supervise them even more strictly. Until things settled down.

Allow me. Allow me to continue. That man. Yes, that man. There. It's him alright. El Hajj Abderrahmane. My . . . yes, that's right . . . my father.

paternal authority = controlling & overbearing
& it's not unshakeable before she leaves the family,
39 she notices the cracks in the wall
and the fallen portrait
of father

ABOVE ALL, DON'T LOOK BACK

My father's turn. Main character. Due to his role as parent and uncontested head of the family, but also due to his portliness. He takes up the entire stage. Close-up of his face distorted with anger. His bloodshot eyes. The quivering of his upper lip. His nervous stuttering, revealing unusual dismay.

Without further delay, foreseeing the considerable damage that The Disappearance could cause him, he would take control of the situation. I think that he would be the one to make the most sensible proposal. The plan that everyone had been feebly awaiting.

He looks around for an ashtray. My mother runs. He crushes his cigarette and takes a moment to catch his breath. He's going to talk. It's his turn.

"Why not spread a version of the story that is more 'suitable,' considering the situation? Suitable for individuals of our rank, our status. For I can already see them now . . . sneering . . . exchanging their looks. No! Amina was kidnapped. It was an abduction. It's a growing trend these days, it's credible, it's unpredictable, and above all, it's irrefutable. Because . . . because . . . Even if we were to say that we sent her to an aunt's house, to my sister's house in Algiers for example, in the end people would know . . . especially if other people were aware. Of course, none of us have anything to do with it . . . do we?" he says, brutally addressing the remark to my mother, who stops her pacing in midstride. Hundreds of girls have disappeared these past years. Torn from their family by blood- and power-thirsty criminals. Television and newspapers inform the public, exhibiting the unfortunate victims, who are now forever tarnished. Pure, defenseless girls. Above all suspicion. Like our daughters. All of them!

He points menacingly at the two girls crouched together one against the other in the darkest corner of the living room.

"Are all the windows closed? Yes, that is what we'll say. That she was kidnapped. On this very night. That's right . . . and the proof? All her things are still up in her room, untouched. She told us that she was too hot inside the house, so she was going out to the garden for some air. We heard a car engine, car doors slamming, and a scream that was very quickly muffled.

ABOVE ALL, DON'T LOOK BACK

That's all. At first, we thought that it was her brother who had arrived home. And then . . ."

He strokes his mustache. He sits down on an armchair in order to more comfortably contemplate the continuation of the scenario.

"Ah yes, this is definitely the way to go . . . And . . . It's an ill wind that blows nobody any good . . . This will all have a substantial bearing on the electoral campaign. Regardless of what I do . . . And then, we can investigate. Officially. As soon as I am elected. And I swear we will find her again. With or without the help of the police, we will find her."

I don't want to listen to what they are saying about me any longer.

All I am thinking about is the moment when I will arrive.

All I see around me are sweaty faces, empty gazes, and all I hear are hollow words. Every one of them, yes, every one of them so comfortably settled in their own certainty. Is there nothing at all then that can shake them up? Nothing that can make them disappear?

I close my eyes, squeezing my eyelids shut very tightly. As I did when I was a child. I would call it turning off the lights. Fragile and fleeting, bubbles of light appear and disappear in the dark, in the depths of my inner screen. They burst into myriads of magnificent iridescent sparkles when I decide to pursue them with determination.

Fragments of images follow me as well. Accompanied by a terrifying noise, even more terrifying than the rumbling of a thunderstorm or a tumult underground. A tumult that never ends and rings incessantly in my ears. I don't know where it comes from. From within me, no doubt.

Visions.

Hallucinations.

Everything is an illusion. I cannot stop. I must not. I must escape. Keep on walking. My eyes closed. Without seeing. Without hearing. The screams are there once again. The dust. The smoke. The stones. I must continue.

The earth is moving. The ground trembles and I am unsteady on my feet.

I don't want to look at the landscape that is unfolding all around me. I don't want to see the mountains stripped bare, the burning forests. I don't want to see the valleys, the plains, the sterile spaces swept with dust, the cracked earth sprinkled with thorns, the bare trees without leaves, the perpetual, never-changing course of the sun in the sky.

All geography and genealogy have become sterile.

ABOVE ALL, DON'T LOOK BACK

As the bus continues, amid the noise of the motor and the racket that is pounding painfully in my ears, I seem to hear—rhythmically scanned and endlessly repeated—this sentence, in this order: "Run, run, and above all, don't look back."

I think I must have dozed off to these words with my head resting against the windowpane.

It is probably the sound of cars honking, along with the repeated jolts of the bus whenever the driver hits the brakes, that has woken me up. I open my eyes.

The bus is forging a path through very dense traffic. The city lies before us. There is recklessness, disorder, and increasingly visible decrepitude all around. Men and women come and go, completely indifferent to what surrounds them: run-down buildings with deep cracks scarring their façades, walls crumbling down, balconies in utter ruin, caved-in sidewalks, streets etched with potholes, and heaps of rubbish. With their fur standing on end, troops of black cats stroll around like masters of the mounds of debris. A spectacle that is strangely beautiful in the flamboyant and incomparable late afternoon light that is blanketing the roofs.

The bus stops. The driver turns toward me. Before getting off, I bow in his direction. He is a precious witness for me in the future investigation. I point at an unknown young man that I have just spotted leaning up against one of the arcades bordering the avenue.

"Ah, there he is over there! That's him! My cousin Mourad. He's waiting for me. Could you go tell my parents that I arrived okay whenever you get back? I'll call them from my aunt's house, but if you drop by, they'll be completely reassured. May God protect you and yours, Ammi Mohammed. And please don't forget, I'm counting on you!"

As I walk along the avenue, I don't once look at the sea right beside me. I walk for a long time. At first I don't even notice that I am being followed by a couple of scrawny black cats with bristling fur. No doubt the same ones that were walking nonchalantly over the mounds of debris.

In the shared taxi that is taking me to my destination, an elderly woman is sitting next to the driver. She is wearing a white haik that is striped with wide pieces of old-fashioned raw silk. The bottom half of her face is covered by a small, white muslin veil bordered with fine lace. It has been a long time since I have seen a woman wearing this traditional Algerian attire. She seems to be from another time. She turns toward me. She stares at me for a long time. Her eyes are very pale, as though faded, with crow's-feet wrinkles finer than scratches on either side of them. She holds a small carton of orange juice.

"Here, drink . . . drink this, my girl. The place where we are headed might very well resemble hell."

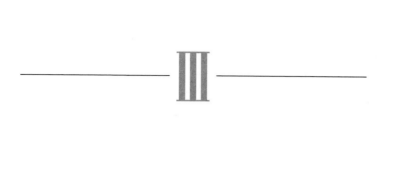

The sky seems to be hanging askew over the ruins. A bit as though it had suddenly shifted, in forty-five seconds. It's as precise as that—less than a minute. But what is one minute in terms of the history of our beautiful planet, the Earth? Not even an infinitesimal fleck of dust, not even the least blink of an eye.

I've looked in vain for explanations—I still can't understand how it is possible that the sky is now leaning a bit too far over this part of the world without anybody showing an ounce of concern.

Men, women, and children wander down the roads littered with vestiges of the disaster sticking up like pieces of broken glass.

They drift along—stunned, haggard, undone. By day and by night.

From time to time, they stop, uncomprehending and unable to stop staring.

And then they go on.

Walking.

Searching.

Road by road. Ruin by ruin.

People say to them: *Mektoub*. It was written.

So they attempt to decipher the signs that are inscribed there: fissures, cracks, crevices, tracks, trenches, scars, gaps. The inscription of emptiness and absence, still obscure for anyone who hasn't lived through this fragment of history.

With hollow, fixed eyes, they attempt—tirelessly and in vain—to decipher the scriptural traces of their pain. To give a meaning back to the present in a place that is no longer. To give a meaning back to this place in a present that is no longer.

It was written.

They walk on.

They keep searching.

They will go on digging.

To the utter limits of pain.

ABOVE ALL, DON'T LOOK BACK

Not me either—I don't know any longer—what is real and what is false, what is legible and what is not.

From now on, I'm not going to talk just about myself. You'll have to accept that. You'll have to understand. I'm going to turn toward others. People whose paths have crossed mine in this strange place, this camp, this receptacle of all suffering and all new beginnings. Please don't be upset with me. This could be how I'll unravel the threads. Because these were the people, the only people, who helped me hold on, who helped me get back on my feet and rediscover what human qualities and sensibility were still left inside me.

When I was in the lycée, reading a variety of books, I discovered how in scientific language there are often a number of words for saying the same thing.

To remain within well-known vocabulary understood by all, the first tendency would be to say: EARTHQUAKE. Some might just say: QUAKE.

In a more scholarly fashion, one would speak of a TELLURIC TREMOR, from the Latin *tellus,* earth. Or else, to maintain the age-old scientific rivalry between Latin and Greek roots, apply the term SEISMIC, from the Greek *seismos,* meaning "to shake."

The whole thing developed, explained, and presented by serious, impressive people, surrounded by apparatus, video screens, and charts. The same people who are on television after every catastrophe. Always the same ones. They use serious, weighty, imposing words, such as Plate Tectonics, Spreading Crack, Landslides, Compressional Wave, Magnitude, Epicenter, Scale, Scars, Faults, Fractures, and, of course, not to be forgotten: Aftershocks. Inevitable, they warn us. Tremors, thousands of tremors of varying intensity, sufficiently numerous, perceptible, and powerful to bring the populace, already traumatized and panicking, out of their homes, and to maintain fear. So that no one will forget.

In human language—simply and basically human—it is an entire other set of words. More direct, more abrupt words, harmful words that leave no room, no crack through which the

ABOVE ALL, DON'T LOOK BACK

Light of Science could filter in: collapse, rubble, death, ruins, desolation, disruption, chaos, anger, helplessness, despair.
And above all, above all: a loss of balance, insanity.
Annihilation.
End-of-the-world words. The end of a world.

Every night, between each tremor duly recorded by the seismographs and classed the next morning as mild aftershocks, Nadia dreams that she can almost touch the sky with her fingertips, if it will just tip a bit more.

Dadda Aïcha keeps moaning in her sleep. From time to time, she speaks. But we can't understand what she is saying. She claims to be uttering incantations to ward off jinn who are lurking around us.

There is also the nearby barking of dogs who prowl about the periphery of the camp—disoriented, starving, stimulated by the persistent stench of corpses—and who, having been kicked off their own territories, can't even stray about anymore through the now overpopulated vacant lots.

Ever since he was asked to live with us in our tent, Mourad has slept lengthwise across the door. Or rather the opening that serves as a door. He trusts no one. We can go on saying that there is nothing worth stealing, but it makes no difference. He won't listen to us. Every evening, before going to sleep, he inspects the surrounding area and walks around our little stronghold again and again. He has secured the tent panels with huge blocks of stone. These weren't very hard to find; it was carrying them all the way here that was difficult. He had to ask neighbors for help. Then, almost all the new tent dwellers ended up doing the same thing. It was just a matter of someone thinking of it. Lacking furniture, the stones serve as ledges for arranging our things. We keep the blankets and dishes there. On one of them, Dadda Aïcha has put a yellow plastic tablecloth with a blue pattern on it and a jug of flowers. Red and pink plastic flowers that she found, not too far away from here, on a pile of garbage. Naturally, she washed them off first. She says colors liven up your life. Even if.

She was also the one who found me lying lifeless on the road—curled up, ice-cold, stiff—so stiff that at first she thought there was nothing that could be done for me, that I was gone.

ABOVE ALL, DON'T LOOK BACK

That is how she says it. She never uses the word "dead," but talks about a departure, a great journey. When she leaned over me, she could see that I was still breathing. So she spoke to me. Softly. In the hollow of my ear. She spoke for a long time. A very long time. She forced me to drink a bit of water, drop by drop, like you get a baby to drink. Later on, she admitted that it had taken many long hours and a great many words to get me to come back, to keep me here.

I don't know what she said to me. She has never wanted to tell me.

When she knew that I had heard her, she decided she would bring me here. Naturally, she wasn't able to carry me herself. She sat down next to me and waited. Two young men walked by. She called them over.

Dadda Aïcha has never really known her age. She is definitely very old. Over eighty, at least. All you need do to be convinced of this is take one look at her gnarled knuckles and deeply wrinkled face. And when you listen to her, to the fragments of her story, or at least the ones she is willing to share with us, you can go a long way back in time. All the same, she has a self-assured way about her, a perfectly straight back, along with a surprisingly supple body, and more energy than many women far younger in appearance. And above all, she never complains. People sense in her a tremendous ability to cope with adversity and all the suffering that comes with it. A sort of long-standing familiarity with hard times.

When the earthquake hit, she was in Ammi Mohamed's little grocery store. She always did her own shopping. Before her building was marked with a red X and scheduled for demolition forcing her to move out, she was living alone in a furnished room at the far end of a garden, a few meters from the house where she had once been employed as a general maid. After having her retire, her employers allowed her to finish her days where she had always lived. A room that was in very bad shape, as she says, but a roof over her head all the same. She wouldn't have known where else to go. In exchange, she continued to render them occasional service and to look after the garden. She loved that more than anything else. All around her little home she had planted mint, coriander, parsley, and even some tomatoes. She talked to the trees and flowers. And she swears they would lean over to listen.

She no longer has a house. And her employers' house caved in as well. There is nothing left at all. Once, it was a sprawling residence built by farmers during the colonial period: a time when the region was nothing but farmland and tiny villages of several dozen souls each. Her own mother had worked there earlier. And at a very young age, Dadda Aïcha was hired as well.

After Independence, the new occupants of the house—the family of a high-ranking civil servant of the brand new Algerian

ABOVE ALL, DON'T LOOK BACK

Republic—agreed to keep Dadda Aïcha on as their servant. But in the house, everything was rapidly falling to ruin. The walls. The roof. The foundation. Everything was wearing away, coming apart, almost before their very eyes, as if gnawed away by some mysterious force. Only the trees stood firm. Trees more than a hundred years old. Because, as she explained to us once, trees are the only beings in this world, and perhaps in the entire universe, to have the marvelous ability to develop roots that push deep into the earth.

The ground has shaken.

Without delay, the ancient chorus inflects the indignant cry, articulates it loud and clear:

"O ye men and women, actors and witnesses in this time of impiety and blasphemy! The world is shaking! Don't you see a sign in that? A sign of God's reproof! We must accept this just punishment from God the All-Powerful, the Compassionate! Fear God! Fear his wrath! Plead for his forgiveness! Bow down! Let us expiate together as one! But above all, let us thank God for his boundless mercy!"

In this place where you expect prayers and contemplation, men and women gathered together in grief—unified, dignified, and restrained—there is nothing other than superstitions, curses, threats, and outbursts.

I had a dream last night. A strange and pervasive dream.

It was much more than a dream, a vision really. I saw a scene and it was so exact that I found myself instantaneously projected out of time. When I woke up, a feeling of well-being veiled my anguish, as if softening the violence of the invocations and appeasing the angry rumble of people hurling imprecations that could not really calm anything down, and seemed simply to be trying to muffle the growling and heaving of the earth.

An old man sits facing a little girl who is none other than me; I am sure of it. Then, in a strange split from myself, I am able to look at them both.

We are in a patio, near the door to a large room. He is seated on a mattress covered with shimmering green fabric. All the doors opening on this white-tiled inner courtyard are open. It is a very hot day.

Who is he? I don't know. I don't know anymore. Nor do I know where we are.

As a little girl still ignorant and unsuspecting, I am looking at him. He doesn't seem to know I am there. I remain still. I hold my breath so I won't disturb the serenity emanating from this place and moment.

Dressed in an impeccable white *gandoura,** he is softly chanting. A book is open on his lap. With gilt letters on a shiny green leather cover, perhaps polished through use. It is the Qur'an, the book that only he is allowed to touch. He isn't reading it. With his eyes half-closed, he is reciting verses without even glancing down at the pages, which he turns from time to time.

The little girl doesn't take her eyes off him.

In his right hand he is fingering black wooden beads, which he slides with a regularity that fascinates her. The muted sound of his voice resounds throughout every part of the little girl's body, as she remains motionless in the corner of the room, and it gradually makes all the other household noises fade away. Letting herself be lulled, she grows sleepy at this moment and closes her eyes, just as a slight buzzing sound comes to her like the hissing of a fire very close by and yet out of reach. As he utters words, she is able to grasp their gentle warmth, but doesn't understand their meaning. Words full of fervor. Words that remain suspended in the silence, twirl about in spirals, and paint arabesques below his lowered eyelids.

How she would have liked to know how to read, to repeat along with him in that tone at once gentle and firm, the phrases of his slow recitative, flowing out and disappearing into the exquisite purity of the summer sky, a recitative that—and this she knows—opens the doors to paradise!

It is just a vision. I know that.

I am totally absorbed in this place, at this moment—I am bathed in tenderness and light. Beams of pure light spread all around me in waves that roll, unroll, change directions, spread, and rise slowly to the sky. I sense vibrations, inside me, inside this dream, at this very moment.

*A loose short-sleeved tunic worn in North African countries. —TRANS.

It was the women who first made the place their own very quickly, as if they had always known similar uncertainty, lived in similar conditions.

Within several hours, they had marked out their territory with so much determination that even the most hardy men had to step back.

Before setting up on the land recently cleared for disaster-stricken families, the women stood with their hands on their hips, keeping one eye on the belongings they had managed to salvage and the other on their offspring, and assessed elements of the situation. First of all, the distribution of tents. The amount of space to be attributed to each one in relation to the number of family members. The overall layout and arrangement of neighboring tents. Forty tents per camp. Forty families. There was indeed some hesitation before things got underway. Before the mad dash. Should people be grouped together by class, social status, or origin? Or should they simply re-create the old neighborhoods, one house at a time, one building at a time? Affinities were very quickly established without the intervention of any official authorities. Those responsible for the distribution and organization of supplies were very rapidly overwhelmed. But the cleverest folk didn't waste time asking a lot of questions. They just set up without delay.

Sent ahead to reconnoitre, an incredible number of incredibly excited children arrived in the camps from all over and dispersed like "thickly scattered moths"* even before assignments began to be announced. When the evening came, some people even had a hard time evicting children who were not their own—youngsters who, without their families taking notice, had managed to find safe haven in a tent and then refused to leave it. Serenity returned with the night and the darkness that invaded the grounds. A few car headlights were left on so that latecomers could settle in.

*Comparison borrowed from a verse in the Qu'ran about the resurrection [sura 101: "A day wherein mankind will be as thickly scattered moths / And the mountains will become as carded wool," verses 4 and 5].

ABOVE ALL, DON'T LOOK BACK

In the middle of the night, men, women, and children rushed out of their tents screaming after the first nocturnal aftershocks, which were always more disturbing than ones in broad daylight. Nobody had really come to accept the idea that there was nothing to fear under a tent, that you are protected. At least from dangers that come from within the earth.

As early as the first day, in an attempt to keep up some semblance of family intimacy, there appeared enclosures—made of reeds, branches, and occasionally even pieces of cardboard picked up here and there—around the tents. Also pegs were stuck in the ground, clotheslines strung up, and wide expanses of cloth hung over areas of common turf. The cloth was of every color and description: canvas, old sheets, blankets, and other pieces of fabric scavenged from among the ruins. Not only to offer protection from the sun but also to annex off a maximum amount of space, for no one intended to let neighbors encroach on their lot. Then, since there was no proper way of storing one's belongings, the most eclectic mix of utensils, colorful plastic basins, camp stoves, woven mats, buckets, and brooms slowly accumulated in front of each tent. Not to mention the mattresses and blankets that were aired out first thing in the morning and left out in the sun for the whole day to get rid of odors.

Little by little, life returned in full force. The clamor of voices, the smell of food cooking on the stove, the scent of detergent, the cries and chaotic scampering of the children, the increased frequency of visits from family, and fewer and fewer incursions of official delegations always to be received with proper decorum, the invasion of determined squadrons of voracious, insatiable mosquitoes, whispers and sighs throughout the suffocating night, anger and long expanses of silence during the exhausting afternoon heat, gossip and unjustified accusations, resentment fading as quickly as it flares, alliances and outright disputes, insults and reconciliation, controversies, confrontations and displays of friendship, men's domino games, moonlit evenings with songs hummed softly, very softly, as if out of fear of creating a shock or awakening fresh wounds, and noisy mornings with their variously tuned radios engaging in musical duels: rai* versus Andalusian music, French pop versus Kabyle songs.† Followed by the recorded voices of the preachers, booming out powerfully, from one end of the camp to the other, reciting the Qur'an and delivering ardent sermons.

A situation of overcrowding that was more or less calmly accepted because it was considered to be temporary, with everyone holding on to a deeply ingrained hope of finding a real house again as quickly as possible. A place where you could shut the doors, close the blinds, and be isolated behind thick solid walls that blocked out noise, a place with enough space, on solid enough foundations, a place where you could re-create what a home was all about and enjoy the privacy perceived by everyone as the ultimate luxury.

---

*A highly popular Algerian musical genre, featuring synthesizers, drum machines, and lyrics in French and Arabic. —TRANS.

† Songs from the Berber-speaking people inhabiting mountainous regions of northeastern Africa. —TRANS.

At present, there are four of us living in this tent. Dadda Aïcha has brought us here one after another. Nadia was the second to arrive. After the evening of the earthquake, she was homeless. She wandered through the streets all day and took shelter in a neighbor's courtyard for the night. She hid when she saw the teams responsible for picking up women and children with no roof over their heads, no family, no guardian. She didn't want to be too far from her house, or at least the spot where it had stood, a couple of hours earlier, a couple of days before. One night, she wasn't able to find a place to go. Her neighbors had gone off to live elsewhere, joining their family. She was left all alone and terrorized by the idea of having to find a place to hide for the night. She went and stood in front of the entrance to the camp. Dadda Aïcha happened to be passing by there. She took her by the hand. And since then, she has lived with us.

Nadia is almost seventeen years old.

She was supposed to start the lycée this year. She was going to submit her registration forms. She was supposed to be in first year. She was supposed to sign up for scientific studies. She was supposed to take private lessons to catch up in math and the sciences. Her mother had been adamant about it. But a large section of the lycée collapsed, just like the elementary schools and most of the collèges in the region. Whether new or decrepit, all the buildings have been seriously damaged without distinction. So Dadda Aïcha takes the bus into the city almost every day to ask about Nadia's registration. Nadia has no relatives here anymore. She thinks that maybe she doesn't have any relatives at all. Up to now, nobody has come to take her away or to make sure that she is still alive. She doesn't have any official documents either. No report cards, no school certificates. Everything has disappeared under the rubble. But Dadda Aïcha is obstinate. Stubborn as a mule. Nadia will be starting school the moment the lycée reopens its doors. She swears it to herself. For her part, Nadia doesn't complain too much about her extended holiday. In the meantime, Dadda Aïcha has been bringing her books. All the books she can manage to find when she goes out scavenging for objects that could be useful and, above all, make this place we live in look more attractive. Since she doesn't know how to read, she brings home anything that vaguely corresponds to the idea she has of Science. Often complete rubbish. Books on mechanics, electronics, and medicine. She says that Nadia might use them some day, that it makes no difference, and they have to be kept like treasures. She brings me some as well, paperbacks, in pretty bad shape for the most part. The sort that you find piled up on the ground at the improvised markets that have arisen all over the outskirts of our devastated cities. Books that are willingly given to her for free, since there is pretty much no one who would dream of buying them. And seeing that she doesn't want me reading just any old book, she chooses them according to the pictures on their covers.

But I don't understand what has been happening to me since I got here. The words I decipher resist me fiercely. Characters elude me. Plots get muddled. Sometimes it even happens that the strands just slip right through my fingers, and it is like the stories are unraveling, stitch by stitch, as I try to enter their alternate worlds, their invented universes. It is perhaps due to the fact that what I've been experiencing, what I've been seeing since I came to this camp, seems a lot more extraordinary, a lot more extravagant, than anything I could have read up until now or anything others could have invented before me.

In a similar way, when I wake up in the morning, it takes me a long time to put the pieces of my story back together. To figure out exactly where it is that I am, and to integrate myself back into reality. It is as though a jinni—a cunning little spirit, one of those Dadda Aïcha thinks she sees lurking around us— were taking advantage of the time when I sleep to torment me, to scatter my dreams in disparate shards, and to hold me back at the break of day so that I can't open up my eyes fully and move toward the light.

Dadda Aïcha has been out looking all around the camp in search of teachers for Nadia. It is Mourad, who has been here ever since day one, helping most of the earthquake victims get

ABOVE ALL, DON'T LOOK BACK

set up, who tells her where to find a math teacher and a science teacher too. Not very far from here, in Camp 6. Indeed, I
wonder what we would do without him. From the beginning,
he has been able to make himself indispensable.

Mourad is fifteen years old. He looks a lot older, despite being short. His face with its all-too-visible signs of a precocious, too precocious maturity, his reactions to things, his way of speaking and the words he so rarely chooses to utter are not those of an adolescent. He is among the many here, especially during these troubled times, who have skipped directly from being a child to being an adult. Their gazes have been sharpened by a steady onslaught of misery, humiliation, and violence of the least acceptable, least tolerable sort. From his childhood, all he carries with him are wounds—still fresh, no doubt, despite his overconfident attitude. He never talks about it. Nor does he talk about his family. Nobody knows where he comes from. He has been out of school for a long time now. The one evening when he let down his guard a bit, the only thing he told us was that he had left his village and parents when he was twelve, after being kicked out of elementary school. When Dadda Aïcha first met him, he was already living in the camp. With some cardboard boxes and a couple of planks of wood, he had built himself a night shelter next to one of the fences.

To survive, he runs errands for anyone who asks: he transports jerricans of water for various people; guards tents when the occupants have to go take care of administrative matters; stands in line for elderly people when the food distribution truck arrives. He is ingenious and has no equal when it comes to repairing appliances, assembling things, and installing television antennas. And TV is an essential distraction for anybody who is here, man, woman, or child. That is why people tolerate his being around. Otherwise everyone is on their guard, ever since we realized that there are thieves and con artists of every possible description dwelling in the camps, hoping to make use of their talents in what could be described as ideal conditions, given the distress and vulnerability of the survivors.

Mourad, for his part, has known how to make sure he is accepted, even appreciated by the earthquake victims. Occasionally, when parents ask him, he even babysits for them. He really loves the littlest kids. He knows how to keep them distracted. He enthralls them with magic tricks. I have no idea who taught him how to make cards vanish, to make scarves reappear, to snatch watches from people's wrists and objects from the very pits of pockets without the person thus deprived noticing a thing. Let no one dare call him a thief though! He never stole anything from anyone.

There is one thing he has never wanted to do. That is accept money in exchange for retrieving objects or personal belongings of former inhabitants right out from the middle of the rubble, as many young people will do here. Two of his buddies, who had also come from elsewhere, had made a deal with a woman: they were to hunt for a jewelry box buried under the rubble, in exchange for a large sum of money. In a matter of seconds, they were swallowed up at the precise moment when, just as the woman had told them to do, they were working their way into a hollow space between two concrete posts that were unstably balanced under a flagstone. The aftershock was very strong. It finished off the job already underway. No one was able to extract them from their tomb.

One evening, Dadda Aïcha came home late. She had waited in line for two hours at the supplies center for five kilograms of semolina. Mourad walked her all the way home. It must be said that the nights are very dark. It's like we are all wrapped in mourning. The two floodlights set up at the entrance of each camp, though very powerful, are not enough. And thanks to numerous technical glitches, the camp is often plunged in darkness. When she is by herself, Dadda Aïcha never feels particularly at ease. And yet, she claims that at her age there is nothing left to fear, not even death, since it has already begun to infiltrate, to spread slowly, like a kind of vermin that starts with the extremities and sabotages each bodily function one at a time. All the same, Dadda Aïcha is afraid of being attacked, despite the presence of guards who patrol until the break of day. As for Nadia and me, she won't let either of us walk alone after the shadows begin to throw off the chains the day attached to their ankles. That's the way she talks.

That same night, Mourad came in with her. He joined us

for dinner. He sat a little bit off to the side. He ate. Then, without saying a word, Dadda Aïcha went and got a blanket. She placed it on one of the foam mattresses that she had managed to acquire thanks to the generosity of a regional merchant who had come all the way here himself, to hand out his donations. Pointing to a corner of the tent, she designated a place. His place. Mourad didn't say anything either. He just pulled the mattress over so that it blocked the entrance.

Dadda Aïcha wakes up many times during the night to check if he's still there. She says that it's possible he'll take off one of these days or nights. Without even knowing where he's headed. She's certain of it. She says you can't hold back someone like him. He can't really be tamed. Except with love. She also says that one is never sure if they love enough or know how to love someone in such a way that they feel the need to put down roots. So she takes care of him. In her own way. Just as she cared for her flowers, her herbs, and her trees. She talks to him. And he listens to her. She compares him to a golden thistle because of the color of his hair, or else a wildcat who is at once distrustful and endearing, and above all very independent. Before serving our meals, she waits until he gets home. She won't let us start without him. Even when he is a bit late joining us. She never asks him questions. She waits until he feels like talking. In the beginning, we had the impression that he was always on the point of leaping to his feet, always on the lookout. As if he were wound up, ready to spring at any moment. Now he seems more at ease. More trusting. Almost stable, almost stabilized. His gaze has lost a bit of its sharpness. Nadia spends a lot of time discussing things with him. He doesn't always respond. Sometimes, right in the middle of a conversation, he just gets up and leaves. As if suddenly lacking air and needing to breath. But he always ends up coming back. And every night, he brings something home with him. More often than not, a contribution to dinner. He has never said it, but it is clear he wouldn't want to be considered a parasite. In all places and at all times, he always wears this harsh, barely masked look of distrustful, easily wounded pride.

Dadda Aïcha doesn't always answer the questions we ask her. She doesn't really like talking about herself. She prefers telling stories. Stories of bygone days. Stories that grandmothers love telling.

I like listening to her, especially when she talks about the French. She knows the *roumis** well. She lived with them for a long time. She speaks their language fluently, since she grew up with her boss's daughters. She even knows a few words in Spanish. At one time, the foreman of the property was Spanish. Today we have a hard time imagining all these foreigners living in this country and making themselves at home. Even if their language has stayed with us. But Dadda Aïcha seems to miss those days. Certain aspects of those days, she adds immediately, afraid we might imagine that she was recalling a lost paradise. She says that there were injustices of course, and there was discrimination too, it can't be denied, but there was also an art of living, a real love of nature that no longer exists. Nowhere on Algerian soil. I don't really know what that means. I'm not sure if the two go together. I mean injustice and a love of nature. I think she must be exaggerating a bit. Maybe she's talking about trees and flowers. She says that today there is nobody left who really loves flowers. That you hardly ever see them on apartment balconies or on terraces. No more than you can see flower gardens around villas, because they keep putting up higher and higher walls to keep out passersby. Now wrought-iron bars, metal cisterns, and satellite dishes are all that can be seen. So maybe that is why the earth feels so neglected.

The first time she asked me if my grandmother told me stories too, I felt as though a tremendous gulf opened up inside me and sucked me down into it. Then I replied that I didn't know. That I didn't even know if I'd ever had a grandmother. Or even a family.

*Algerian term for the French, or for Europeans in general (from "Roman"). —TRANS.

ABOVE ALL, DON'T LOOK BACK

From time to time, abruptly during a pause in our conversation, she slips in a question or a remark. For no obvious reason. And she waits. But I'm not so quick to react now. In those moments, she has a sparkle in her eye. It's as if she were trying out names. It's become a game now. Even Mourad joins in when he's around. At first, he would only call me the names of various fruits or flowers, just for fun. I treasured them. It pleased me to be called Plum or Jasmine, Cherry or Gillyflower.

They call me when I've got my back turned, or else when I'm plunged deep in a book. They hope that if I hear my name, they'll get a reaction. So they're always trying, at all times of the day. Dadda Aïcha is convinced that the important thing is to name me. To help me find my original identity. That the rest will no doubt follow. It is simply a matter of causing a stir, like tossing a stone into a pond. Then, there is a chance that the first word will surface, the one that names, designates, and distinguishes us. The one that is sewn onto the very skin of our most distant memories. Even if that skin is now in shreds, broken up by too many scrapes, too many wounds. That is what she keeps repeating. She firmly believes it is true. The first days, she would call me every five minutes. She began with the most common names. The most old-fashioned, scoffed Nadia. "Come on, Dadda Aïcha, she doesn't look like a Messaouda at all. Nor a Saada, Saadia, Fatma, Zohra, or even a Fatma-Zohra!"

Without worrying about this objection, Dadda Aïcha continues running through all the names of people who have been important in her life. Her mother was called Yamina. Her sisters, Mouna and Fatima.

For some time now their repertoire has been expanding, thanks to Mourad. He always has a little scrap of paper handy for writing down the names he hears during the day, and since he is often with children, the lists are long and varied. He has a clear preference for names with a foreign twang: Sabrina, Célia, Mélissa, Inès, or more exotic still, Tanya, Ludmilla, or Syrine—names that stand out shockingly in the state civil registries. The latest in the world of naming. Knowing his desire to leave for distant horizons, faraway shores he imagines to be more clement, I think he must take the time to select those names himself, before coming to us with his suggestions.

The doctor who examined and questioned me the first day asked Dadda Aïcha to let me be the one to choose my own name. It will only be a temporary name though, he said. Just for the time being, while we wait. According to him, it was the process that was important. He said it could be a first step toward self-recognition. Or was it rebirth? I don't recall. But I couldn't make up my mind. All the names I thought of reminded me of something or someone. And I didn't want to be confused with some other girl. A girl with a past behind her already, a history, with dreams and future plans. I would have liked for a brand-new name to be invented for me, and me alone.

For a long time, Dadda Aïcha simply called me *Benti*, my girl. Nadia and Mourad, for their part, improvised all sorts of names, depending on my mood, their mood, and their sources of inspiration. We had a lot of fun. Then, one night when I was standing there in front of her, Dadda Aïcha simply made the decision. She looked me up and down, from head to toe, for a very long time. It was as if she was looking for some particular quality in my eyes, my face, in every part of my body. No doubt an answer to the questions plaguing her ever since day one. Ever since that moment when she had found me alone, lying lifeless on the road. A shiver passed through my body, and I tried to meet her gaze. With great difficulty. I felt searched, pierced through by that gaze which was so straight, so direct. By those pale eyes, so pale, as though faded by too much grieving, too many trials. To me it felt like this went on for a very long time. Then she took my hands, held them firmly between her own, and said with great simplicity:

"For the time being, you will be called Wahida. First and unique, but also alone. Simply because at the instant I found you, you seemed to me totally, irreparably alone. Yes, from

ABOVE ALL, DON'T LOOK BACK

now on, and maybe for a long time to come, you will be Wahida to us. For now, while we wait."

Without any other certainty, I love and accept this idea of being the first and unique one, and solitude doesn't frighten me at all.

One night Mourad brought us photocopies of illustrated pamphlets that foreign first-aid workers had distributed all over the camp. The document was written in two languages: French and Arabic. It gave recommendations concerning what to do in case of an earthquake. Recommendations that were coming to us a bit too late, but could still be useful if we happened to be housed again elsewhere in several months' time, or in several years.

Using Scotch tape, Nadia had posted a copy near the entrance of the tent. This way everyone can benefit from it, she said ironically. She underlined the first sentence with a red marker and punctuated it with a bunch of exclamation points:
"Where you are doesn't matter!"

"That's right," she said, outraged, "where you are really doesn't matter. Even if you're in a new apartment in a recently constructed housing project that's less than five years old, and that you're living there with such trust, with such naïveté and don't think even for a minute that the foundations under your feet could be rotten, that the concrete, cement, and who knows what else have been tampered with or whatever! That the pillars, indeed all the parts of the structure, are as fragile as a house made of dirt and twigs, while the whole building has passed inspection, been checked over and certified by state officials—officials who are about as conscientious as they are honest when they say it meets safety standards! Yes, that's right! It doesn't matter!"

Here is what could be read in the document:

WHAT SHOULD YOU DO DURING AN EARTHQUAKE?
Where you are doesn't matter. You can expect that the ground or floor will begin to vibrate violently.
1) Shelter yourself immediately.
2) If you can't find shelter, crouch down and protect

your head and face to avoid being wounded by debris or shards of glass.

3) Stay in a protected area until the tremor passes.

4) Be prepared for subsequent tremors or aftershocks. These may occur during a certain period of time after the initial earthquake.

The rest of the pamphlet concerned items that you should have with you for this type of catastrophe, basic first-aid procedures, rescue dogs and their training, and the safest method for freeing victims buried under rubble.

Before photocopying the pamphlets, someone had penned in the following injunction at the very top of the list of recommendations, in large letters, in both French and Arabic, preceded by the number one:

1: Before doing anything else, repeat the declaration of faith many times over:

"There is no God except God, and Mohammed is his prophet."

Because of the exceptional nature of the circumstances in which we find ourselves and the urgency of the situation, many foreigners have been coming to see us. They are part of the missions especially dispatched by states, organizations, and humanitarian associations from all over the world.

First to arrive were the rescue squad workers accompanied by their rescue dogs. Then, more organized, better equipped teams joined them. Day by day, the manpower increased. Among its ranks: journalists, doctors, and psychologists. Many of them men and women sent by humanitarian organizations. But a few came alone, by their own means, without anyone having assigned them to it, out of simple solidarity, simply to lend their expertise.

There have also been politicians, those *"steadfast friends of Algeria throughout this period of terrible suffering that has once again struck its population, already harshly tried by a decade of misfortune,"* as recalled the set phrases rehashed ad nauseam in newspaper articles.

They travel in groups; small groups that are always surrounded by gendarmes or plainclothes police officers brandishing walkie-talkies like weapons to intimidate those who might underestimate their authority. They are guided, oriented, taken for walks around the camps. Sometimes they come to talk with us. And in all the camps there are many disaster victims who await them intently, keen to complain about their living conditions. They come out of their tents or loiter at the bend of an alleyway. They grab the aid workers by the arm and express their grief with such vehemence that it almost seems aggressive, before being firmly, and sometimes brutally, pushed aside by the gendarmes. Misled by their grief, some even go as far as asking for visas in order to be properly cared for. Somewhere else, anywhere, as far away as possible from this country that has known—they declare—only calamities and disorder ever since men claimed, in the name of God, the right to life and death over children, women, and other men. Of course, this is only one version of what supposedly caused the natural disaster we have just lived through. Admittedly, this version is not widely circulated among a population that is more receptive to alternate explanations.

Others, not even considering the fact that there were officers of law and order present, virulently dismissed the Representatives of Civil and Military Authority who dared to accompany the delegations. Outcries and demands for justice erupted from almost every direction. At these times, the national television station's cameras would turn away.

The foreigners always act attentive and curious. About everything. This was especially true of the women. There was even one who, the day after having visited us in the company of an official delegation, had dozens of packages of disposable sanitary pads delivered to us. Her attentiveness was particularly touching and extremely useful. Only a woman would think of that.

Dadda Aïcha told me that, despite the shattered roads and hampered flow of traffic, hundreds of citizens rushed here immediately, even before the civil protection units had arrived. As soon as news of the extent of the catastrophe was known, they came through the night, bringing emergency supplies, shovels, and picks sometimes, from all corners of the country, by car, by truck, or by bus, ready to perform first aid and evacuate all those who needed medical help. They were the ones who took it upon themselves—along with survivors, firefighters, and military personnel—to clear away ruins, often using their bare hands, to remove buried people from the debris. Many a life was saved thanks to them. And in the dark of the night that covered the city, the shining car and truck headlights proved to be very effective. Then they set up makeshift hospitals where volunteer doctors from all over provided emergency care.

When international solidarity got underway, teams were flown in by airplane, bringing blankets, provisions, and tents. Ambassadors were even asked to hand them to us in person, before the lights and cameras of the entire world and the applauding crowds of enthusiastic supporters summoned in for

ABOVE ALL, DON'T LOOK BACK

the occasion, as always, along with Representatives of Civil and Military Authority, who made a special point of coming from the neighboring town or capital. In the parcels that they distributed, there were also diapers for babies, toys and books for kids. Everything had to be thought of!

Foreigners continue to come. Always escorted. Some of them have told us that they aren't allowed to go too far or to walk around alone. They are accompanied everywhere. People fear for them. For their security. They have been warned of the dangers. It is better to watch over them attentively. Police officers hold back swarms of children who start running as soon as they see the visitors, and follow them wherever they go. Not only to be captured on film as they hop around behind them and make faces in the background of the televised news. But mostly because, since they were born during the bloodiest years that this country has ever known—and it has known a fair share—the majority of these children have never seen foreigners elsewhere than on a TV screen.

They call us disaster victims.

I dislike this term, with its undertones of sadness, death, and catastrophe. To everyone we are "the disaster victims of Camp 8." Among the privileged, since they almost immediately installed electricity and two large water cisterns for us, presumably adequate to satisfy our needs. It is our camp that they show on television first. Our camp that they arrange to be visited most of the time. When the cameras roll, everyone comes running. Here, at Camp 8, most of the people didn't know each other before we were all herded together. Not everyone is from the village, nor even from the region. Several families quickly arrived, without baggage or papers. Sometimes even from very far away. Dadda Aïcha has made her inquiries. The possibility of being allocated housing is stronger than the pain of being uprooted.

General consensus has it that ours is the best organized of all the camps. And if you don't fuss too much over details, the grounds are indeed relatively clean. You must simply avoid, if at all possible, going over to the side of the camp where the communal toilets are. It is there that one may best gauge the extent of the disaster.

Teams of psychologists from the capital make rounds of all the camps. They have set up "centers for psychological recovery." They have plenty of work here. And they have a lot of experience, since they have already worked with the survivors of large-scale massacres in neighboring villages. They ask many questions. They really try their best to get survivors to talk. From the youngest to the oldest. But I don't really believe in the virtue of discourse extracted in this manner. When the pain is too deep, it is not merely through words that you will get at the roots of it. Even if, in the case of an earthquake, the causes and circumstances surrounding people's trauma may seem obvious.

And then when it comes to the game of making up stories, one can get good, really good at it. One can always make things

up. Invent, tell lies, pretend. Especially in such circumstances.
This is a unique opportunity to clear the slate, to reinvent one-
self, wouldn't you agree?

They believe in it. They say they are there to help us reach
the point where we will be able to put our feelings in words.
They call it "verbalizing." They ask us to describe our dreams,
they note things down, they get children to take tests and draw
pictures. To help them rebuild themselves after the shock, they
say. But people here would prefer that we talk to them about
repairing and rebuilding houses instead.

You have to sign up with a representative at the town hall
in order to get canned goods, pasta, milk, flour, semolina, blankets, and bottles of mineral water.

Sometimes there are fights when bread and hot meals
are being handed out. The cleverest folks always manage to
get more than the others. And plenty of goods labeled "humanitarian aid" are sold at the markets and boutiques of the
neighboring town. Blankets—donated by the Red Cross or Red
Crescent, flown in by airplanes arriving from many countries—
are in great demand and they sell very well too.

Dadda Aïcha's decision to declare us to the camp administrator to get us added to the census and victim assistance was the beginning of our problems.

How to go about saying who we are? None of us officially exists. And Dadda Aïcha is not our grandmother. We have no real relationship with her. We are just three lost dogs with no collars.

In reality, we don't have any right to occupy a tent. Tents are reserved for families with children. I wonder how Dadda Aïcha was able to get one and, in addition, to move into it with us. I think it was Ammi Mohammed the grocer, her old neighbor, who must have put in a good word for her. He is camp chief now; more specifically, he is responsible for the distribution of provisions.

Once again Mourad took charge. One night he arrived with a big envelope containing various papers. Without any explanation, he placed it on the little table where we were sitting, waiting to eat. Then he sat down close by, in his usual place. Nadia opened the envelope. She read the papers. Declarations of loss. Duly written up, signed, and stamped by a police officer. Legal documents that certified that the three of us were brother and sisters, son and daughters of the late Mohammed Yacine, himself the husband of Fatiha Bent Yacoub, herself the daughter of Dadda Aïcha.

As Nadia was reading aloud, Dadda Aïcha nodded her head silently, not saying anything either. But you could see that she was very pleased. Her eyes were twinkling like stars, and the corners of her mouth trembled as though she were going to cry. Yes, I am certain that she was pleased to be there in the middle of her family, even if they were in a tent, even if it had been necessary to live through a catastrophe to get there.

I couldn't have thought of a better outcome for my story, don't you think?

Mourad later told us that he hadn't even had to bribe the agent. That dozens of people squeezed into the itinerant administrative offices every day to try and re-create an identity for themselves. Some people knew how to be more convincing than others.

It was in this way that in the span of several days I changed my name, my origins, and my status and became, without too much difficulty, the oldest sibling in a family whose virtual members had exercised the good sense to disappear in body and property on the day of the earthquake.

And Dadda Aïcha, who had never had a husband or a child, officially became our grandmother.

Nadia had an older sister. Her name was Leïla. A beautiful, good, intelligent sister; exemplary, of course, like all young girls who disappear prematurely. She was planning on taking the baccalauréat examination this year. Her mother, Mériem, was a dressmaker. A mild, modest women who was very very charitable; irreplaceable like all women prematurely cut off from the affection of their next of kin. Her father, an unrepentant drinker and womanizer, had abandoned them. He was living with another woman. After the divorce, Mériem and her two daughters had moved into a tiny apartment on the eighth floor of the 110-Unit Housing Project. Things were tight, but they managed to live well. They had everything they needed. Mériem, who had entered the world of dressmaking at a very young age—ten years old, according to Nadia—had no equal when it came to embroidering gold and silver onto the most refined caftans, realizing her magnificent work on traditional dresses, sarouals* and caracos,† indispensable items for the marriage trousseaux of all young girls. In her little apartment, there was never an inch of space to spare.

Nadia doesn't really know why it is that when she wakes up in the morning, even before she has opened her eyes and completely regained consciousness, she feels so bad. Why she greets the day with the instantaneous, inconceivable, unacceptable certainty, tearing at her lungs and making the air she breathes unbearably hot, that her life is due to a mistake.

Nadia never went back to the place where their newly constructed building had stood. Like other buildings in the housing project, it collapsed just as naturally, just as spontaneously, just as easily as a row of standing dominoes is flicked over; those who were at home during the tremor were swallowed up by the earth in a few seconds and buried under layers of concrete

---

*Pants, especially in a large baggy style. —TRANS.
† A traditional Algerian outfit, which usually includes an embroidered velvet vest and a long silky skirt or saroual. —TRANS.

and iron. In place of these buildings, there is today a large vacant lot. It has been leveled by remarkably efficient bulldozers, which roared into action so quickly, for they were determined to erase all trace of life in this area and all proof of murderous irresponsibility on the part of building contractors and real-estate agents, who, to this day, have been left unpunished.

That day, her mother sent her to run some errands for dinner. She bought bread, a liter of milk, a can of tomato paste, and a package of pasta. She didn't forget anything. Coming back from the grocery shop, she stopped by to see a friend who lived in a small house, not far from the stadium. She hadn't intended to stay long. She just wanted to ask her a question about, about . . . she can't remember now. Not at all. They talked for a long time in front of the door and then went to sit in the living room. This room was on the ground floor of the villa, on the same level as the garden where they took shelter right from the very first seconds of the tremor.

At that time of day, a few minutes before the evening news on TV, Nadia should have been home. Her mother didn't allow her to hang around on the streets, or to go to her friends' houses, or to walk beside a boy even if he was a classmate. She never stopped warning her daughters. She was so worried about her reputation! A divorced woman had to be careful not to stir up too many rumors. Especially if she lived alone and had daughters. It was because Nadia did not heed her mother's warnings that she is now safe and sound. And it was the first time that she had disobeyed—involuntarily, she swears, her eyes swollen with tears. It was the one time that she violated the rules set down by her mother. Merely a couple of minutes . . . a couple of minutes . . .

The first days, she couldn't stop repeating through her sobs: I made a mistake, I should have been punished for it. I'm the one who should have been swallowed up by the earth; they, they were pure, they were . . .

Dadda Aïcha allows her to talk. She lets her cry. She just

ABOVE ALL, DON'T LOOK BACK

holds her close and caresses her hair while repeating *mektoub*, my little one, my darling, *mektoub*, everything is written, even before we come into the world . . .

Nadia hiccups: if I had just come home when I was supposed to, if I had left my friend a few minutes earlier, if I hadn't . . .

Here and now, this is the only way that people talk. With ifs. And everyone has their story.

They all start with the same word: if . . .

if I hadn't been called to the phone,

if I hadn't needed bread for dinner,

if I had taken the bus a few minutes earlier,

if I hadn't decided to visit my mother,

if I hadn't stayed to chat with my neighbor, standing on the threshold of the doorway which is on the lower level of the building,

if I hadn't gone down to see my friend to borrow or repay some money,

if my boss hadn't asked me to finish studying a case in order to write up a report,

if I hadn't forgotten my glasses or my briefcase in the car . . .

Every man and every woman has the feeling that they owe their life only to these two letters. Two letters that carry the irrefutable proof of the precarious, fragile nature of life. An "if" that, all things considered, is but a turbulent flow of air, a syllable exhaled within a fricative airstream, the articulation of a hypothesis whose implied conclusion is definitely excluded by the very fact that the hypothesis can be expressed using the first person, and which is but a useless return to the past, to the very moment when everything was turned upside down, in a very short, infinitely short span of time.

Talking among themselves, many people stressed how they had perceived in perfect clarity the disproportionate, shallow, and absurd nature of all that had appeared to them as so essential, so basic, but a few seconds earlier: material acquisitions, hostility and resentment, professional ambition, plans and schemes.

The ground trembled.

Their most resolute certainties were brutally shaken up.

Since then, with regard to the reality of the world around them, they have had the impression of being in a perpetual state of instability. The almost physical impression of advancing on a quivering tightwire. As if they had earthsickness. A great many of them say that they have reevaluated their scale of values. But not for long, which goes without saying. Apart from death, needless to say, nothing is ever irreversible. One can't live forever with remorse and affliction—afraid of the next moment to come.

The first signs of a return to normal came very quickly. From the moment they started dividing up the aid, the donations, and the rebuilding assistance.

Time and the instinct for property are nearly as horrifyingly efficient as bulldozers.

A couple of days ago, Nadia ran into one of her mother's clients. As she describes the scenario to me with a pained look on her face, she realizes that for a long time—even when she would visualize her mother measuring fabric and cutting lengths of it (she can still hear the scissors biting the fabric, she adds) or else down on her knees mending hems in the living room with the bright sunlight flooding in through the open windows—the idea never once occurred to her that there would be no more clients, that she would never again have a place to call home, and that no new bride would ever again wear her mother's creations.

If the young woman hadn't called out to her, Nadia never would have recognized her. She was completely draped in black from head to toe. A barely transparent fabric of the same black covered her face. Her entire face. No opening or Afghani-style strip of gauze at eye level for the gaze to filter out. Just a piece of fabric held in place by a headband of sorts, then drawn back over her shoulders and chest; organdy to be precise, Nadia adds, showing herself the true daughter of a seamstress. A slightly translucent organdy veil, rising and falling to the rhythm of the woman's breathing, occasionally sticking to her lips as she spoke. She was wearing black gloves. Black shoes that could barely be seen, since her garment was so very long. The bottom of her dress, flecked with mud and dust, dragged along the ground. Nadia had never seen an outfit like it before. Not even on the Oriental TV channels found in every household and also in every tent, thanks to the miracle of modern technology at the service of the most retrograde ideas. TV channels that, all day long, through the voices of very presentable persuasive preachers, exhort women to return to the most severe fundamentalist Islamic dress code.

Nadia remembered this young woman to be a very dynamic individual. Once they began talking together, her name came back in a flash: Sarah. The young student who went around in jeans and sneakers, the chatty future bride, her eyes sparkling with life. Madly in love with her fiancé, she would go on and on about his endless number of wonderful qualities whenever she came to try on dresses. Basically a girl with the same hopes, dreams, and preoccupations of all girls at that age, full of smiles and projects.

They stood in front of the high school where Nadia had come to register for classes and they talked for a long time. Nadia admitted to Sarah that she was in a state of despair. She described the feelings of guilt that were torturing her and that she couldn't seem to get past. Sarah listened to her carefully, full of compassion. She then confided that her fiancé had disappeared, ruining all her future plans and destroying all her dreams. She then suggested that Nadia come along with her to some daily meetings held at a friend's place. A discussion group. Thanks to those meetings I've found peace of mind and serenity, she confided in a voice full of emotion and a sort of conviction that really affected Nadia.

Nadia agreed right away to join the women's group. All she wants, she keeps repeating, is to be able to talk with other people. To be heard. To be reassured. She wants someone to lighten her load, which is too heavy to bear, and which fills her nights with nightmares and her days with darkness. It's the only desire she has left.

As they were about to separate, Sarah kissed Nadia on either cheek and held her by the hand. Affectionately. Then, in a spontaneous gesture, she hugged her close. At the same time she slipped a paper into her hand—a tract containing verses from the Qur'an, as well as a passage from a book by the Salafi theoretician El Albani, recommending that women cover themselves to avoid exciting the base instincts that exist in all men, and to avoid attracting divine thunderbolts on the community of believers.

In reading this tract carefully, a person can come to only one conclusion: owing to our treachery, our lack of submission, our spirit of rebellion, and our innate irresponsibility, we women are certainly the cause of the deaths of thousands of innocent people. There is no other explanation. This is obvious: one day we will all be summoned to stand trial for crimes against humanity.

Softly, in the hollow of Nadia's ear, as if telling her a secret, the young woman added: You know what I think? I believe, no, I mean I'm certain, absolutely certain, that God took away everything I loved, everything that was dear to my heart, because I was unworthy. My way of talking, of acting, of dressing . . . And you, if your life has been spared, it is because God, the Omniscient, wanted it this way . . . so that, for the rest of your life, you can be a model of proper behavior and dress, and through this, purge yourself of your wrongdoings and help us purify the world. Otherwise you will never find peace.

Listen. Listen to me. Let me say what I know. What I am.

I reached this world in a whirlwind of dust, on a day full of screaming, of inverted skies, fear, chaos, of collapse and rubble, the day after the end of the world, at the end of an infinitesimal and terrifying contraction of the earth.

Since then, they call me Wahida, the one-and-only and perhaps even the unique. From now on, everything is plausible. Maybe even possible.

I feel new. I am new. Without a story. Without a past. Without a shadow. Without memory.

My memory got lost. Mislaid, disintegrated on the extremities of a city that is now only ash, sand, pebbles.

No dreams, no fears. At the edge of night, I plunge into a space that is empty, deserted, bordered by improbable precipices.

When night begins to come undone, when sky and earth have finally separated, I silently slip into the center of the dark that is slowly releasing its embrace. I lift my arms. I stretch my palms toward the promise of dawn, grasping handfuls of the first murmurs, the first shivers; I greet the birth of the day renewed.

Each morning, even before opening my eyes, I welcome in the bluish air, that hesitant shade of blue, still bathed in opacity.

All around me there flows an almost imperceptible sound that swells into an audible clamor of frightened people who can hardly believe the earth they thought submissive can at will, where it will, and precisely when it will, open up, heave, and spew them out.

But they keep walking.

But they keep planting evil and good all around them. Carelessly.

And they keep on deciding for themselves what is good and what is bad. With arrogance. Blindly.

ABOVE ALL, DON'T LOOK BACK

I listen to their footsteps in the quiet of the morning.

What do I care about the sound of their steps in the mornings that they pervert, and on the earth that they burden with their hope-devouring certainties?

Calls rise, penetrate with clenched fists into the daylight, and their steps are suddenly panicked.

What do I care about their futile way of going in circles?

The earth inscribes the signs of their inescapable defeat on the skin of their lies.

Everything calms down and a voice emerges at long last, propelled along by the wind from the darkest regions tucked away inside me, a voice born from a tiny though terrifying contraction of the earth, which threads through all my fears, all my silences, and tells me to move forward—yes, that's right—move forward. Above all, don't look at them; above all, don't listen to them; above all, don't look back. Move forward and go— keep going to your absolute limit.

But tell me, oh tell me, you who are listening, you who know. Can you hear it? Can you hear me?

Sabrina stayed with us until very late tonight. We sat outside, near the door to the tent. She felt like talking, taking advantage of the cool evening hours, relatively cool anyway, before returning to her mother and niece, who were already fast asleep in the tent next door. They are all she has left now. And here mourning, suffering, and absence have become so ordinary, so banal, that listing and recollecting all the people missing from each family seems inappropriate. Verbs expressing material possession, or belonging to a group—that is to say, belonging to a family where those most essential of emotional bonds are forged over the span of a lifetime—are no longer conjugated, except in their negative or past forms. The past tense for completed events, Nadia stressed one day, speaking of her desire to erase everything and move on.

I had.

I don't have any longer.

I was.

I no longer am.

Sabrina is not her real name. That is just the name she uses in the places where she works. For everyone here—her mother, her niece, and all the people who have befriended her in the camp—she is called Naïma.

Sabrina is her nom de guerre. The war that she is fighting against poverty. With her body, her boldness, and her determination as her only weapons. A body that is very slim, very supple, almost perfectly proportioned; very smooth skin, eyes in between hazel and smoky amber, outlined by lashes that are long and lush. Sabrina is very beautiful. Not many people realize that, for the simple reason that she never goes out without her djellaba. An ample black djellaba that hides her curves, plus a long white muslin veil that completely covers the dark silky mass of her hair, as well as a good part of her face.

She gets up very early in the morning. Every day of the week. She rapidly completes her daily housework, reduced to a minimum in the tent that serves as their shelter. Then she wakes her mother, helps her sit up, gets her to drink her coffee, and changes her before seating her in the wheelchair. Her mother is hemiplegic. When it is not too hot, she positions her outside in the sun. Then she wakes up her niece Anissa, washes her, gets her dressed, and feeds her before walking her next door to the prefabricated shacks that serve as a day care for all the small children waiting for their school to be reorganized. Then she waits for the young woman she has hired to watch over her mother during the day. Before, she didn't have a job. Before, she didn't go out alone. Before, she was under careful surveillance by her brothers, who didn't have jobs either. Her mother, Rahma, provided for the whole family by cleaning houses.

Sabrina is gone for the whole day. Sometimes even at night. But that is unusual; usually she manages to come home, even late at night. As silently as possible in order not to be spotted and reported by the guards posted at the camp entrance.

First, she takes the minibus that serves the neighboring city every hour. She gets off just outside the city, near a particularly calm residential area, where the streets are practically traffic free and often completely deserted. Here, she has located a dead-end road surrounded by well-to-do houses. At the foot of a wall that surrounds a majestic villa, she has dug a hole. Big enough to hide a black plastic bag. She places her djellaba and veil inside. She covers the bag with a large stone.

Then she takes a taxi into Algiers. From there, she continues on to the coast in the west. Thanks to a woman she met one day when she was looking for work—of "a completely different sort," she adds—she now has addresses, meeting places, houses where she is expected, hotels where she has her routines. She stays on the whole afternoon, sometimes even late into the night, before making her way back the same way she came. She never arrives at the camp empty-handed. She brings fruit, yogurt, and various juices she has her mother drink with a straw. She always remembers something for Dadda Aïcha as well. She comes by almost every evening to drop off a plastic bag full of fruit or sweets at the door to our tent, and then she goes off without even waiting for us to thank her.

Nobody ever asks her questions about her job, her working hours, or the places where she goes. She doesn't have to account to anyone. Ever since a recent cerebral vascular accident, her mother, who is very weak, can no longer speak. An accident that was the result of a violent dispute with her oldest son, as Sabrina explained to me. She is content just to give looks of boundless love to her daughter, whenever she sees her arrive home and lean over to give her a kiss on the cheek.

Sabrina never works on Fridays, the day she reserves for bathing her mother and doing the laundry. She heats large kettles of water on a camp stove placed outside her tent. Then she undresses her and tenderly, gently, rubs down her entire body with a washcloth. When she is finished, she calls me to give her a hand turning her over. Then she rinses her off. She dresses her in fresh white clothes. She does her hair, ties a silk scarf around her head, slips a perfumed hankie between her breasts, and props her up on a mattress prepared with fresh sheets.

It is for her mother's sake that Sabrina works. So that she will be able to spend the last of her days in a house that is all perfectly white, a brand new house. Oh, to have a little house of their own, just two or three rooms would be enough! They are just a family of three now anyway. A house with a big bathroom entirely in white, a big bathtub, entirely in white too, and sparkling tiles. Yes, it's essential to have a bathroom. With a huge supply of water in a specially made enclosure underground, with a water tank hooked up to a motor to augment the pressure, ensuring that they would never be short of running water. And there would be large windows in every room, protected by wrought-iron bars, with green shutters and white lace curtains. With a little garden where she could let her mother sit outside on nice days. With a pathway bordered in flowerbeds. Narcissus and daffodils. To make a golden carpet. And a honeysuckle climbing up the façade. For its scent. With a fig tree in the middle of the yard to remind her of the house where she grew up, back in her village.

Sabrina's face lights up when she describes the house that she wants to build for her mother. She has given herself very specific goals, complete with deadlines she promises herself she will meet, no matter what happens. And, most importantly, no matter the price. She has opened an account at the Caisse Nationale d'Epargne et de Prévoyance, and she regularly feeds it with deposits at the end of each week. She will realize her dream. She has made her decision. With no hesitation. She moves ahead, with lucidity and determination, never looking back on the moment that has just gone by.

Day after day, she builds her house. She digs the foundations. Stone by stone, she raises it up. With her body. With her mouth. With her breasts. With her hands. With her belly. With her thighs. With the very soft insides of her thighs. With her legs.

One night, when we were alone, she told me about what she was doing. What she herself calls her job. Her days. Men's gazes rest on her. Men's hands touch her. Men's weight pressing down on her. Men's penises entering her. Their bodies. Their odors. Their secretions. Their words. Their demands.

I can't go any further with this evocation of what Sabrina has to do, what she has to live through. Not out of disgust or modesty, but because of a real inability to imagine or comprehend what it is that could help her to bear what seems to me so unbearable.

The cold, hunger, beatings, and rejection are not forged in my memory. I haven't lived in misery, injustice, deprivation, and humiliation. I believe that I have never been confronted with injuries of that sort. The sort that mark the body far longer, far deeper, than any visible scar.

Her personal rebellion has been fed by all those deprivations.

I know, I just do, don't ask me how . . . My own revolt— my need to wander, to forget—comes from some other place.

ABOVE ALL, DON'T LOOK BACK

These needs have been fostered by too many lies, too much silence, too much rejection of another sort, and, most importantly, by the feeling of never really belonging, no matter where I go.

Sometimes I wonder if there is a scale with a variety of degrees or magnitudes for measuring the depth of a person's suffering, the force of their despair, and the irreversible ravages of hate.

Once everyone around us is asleep and we are left alone, seated together in front of the tent, Sabrina talks about all this. Without shame or false modesty. But instead calmly. Without cynicism. Without bitterness. She is not looking for approval, absolution, or indulgence. She has a strange glimmer in her eyes. An indefinable expression. A shimmer in the heart of the night. Soon, very soon, she will be in her home, with her mother and her little niece who will grow up feeling loved and protected.

Nono came with big news today.

At last! He has managed to find what he has been searching for in vain for such a long time in his characteristically relentless and obsessive way.

A disaster victim living in Camp 9, Nono, whose real name is unknown, was recently an engineer specializing in hydrocarbons. A civil servant working for the all-powerful Société Nationale d'Exploitation des Richesses du Sous-sol. He never went back to work—took a long leave of absence for posttraumatic stress, as he explains quite naturally to anyone who asks—after his house collapsed with his wife and seven-day-old baby boy inside, before his very eyes.

He is well into his forties, has an energetic demeanor, a heavyset body, deeply sunken eyes set off against a still babyish face, and a very full mustache so bushy that it almost completely hides his lips. Distinguishing characteristic: a strong unbearable odor of sweat that always precedes him, announces his presence, and then lingers for a long time in his wake. It is not unusual to hear a thunderously loud "Everyone take shelter!" to signal his arrival. He doesn't seem to notice. He seems totally immune to the teasing and remarks of those who watch him go by.

Every night at the same time, he makes his rounds of the camps, following the same route, always pausing at the same places. Every now and then, he stops to scrutinize the sky and study the behavior of birds in flight, with some anxiety. It has been scientifically proven, he explained once, that only animals are capable of sensing any abnormal activity of the earth.

You never catch him without his briefcase, which he carries around clutched close to his chest. The moment he finds someone to talk to who is less repelled by his odor and better able to cope, he just won't let them go. He's tireless and persistent when it comes to natural catastrophes, and he's especially interested in the precise history of various earthquakes over the ages, right down to the last detail. From the most ancient to the most recent ones. From the legend of the two Colossi that collapsed following violent quakes—the first one representing Helios in Rhodes, and the other one representing Memnon, son of Tithonos and Eos, with its singing stones—to the most recent earthquakes in Tokyo and San Francisco, and before those, the destruction of the Lighthouse of Alexandria (one of the seven wonders of the world) in 1302. Not forgetting the huge earthquake that almost entirely destroyed Lisbon in 1755 and was a source of inspiration for Voltaire, an author he is more than happy to quote.

He is now able to evaluate the intensity of aftershocks almost without error. And through constant reference to the scale named after the famous U.S. seismologist Richter (first name Charles Francis), he feels he knows the man as well as if they had met in person. He explains that he would rather refer to Richter than to the Italian Giuseppe Mercalli, who was less precise in his opinion. He has even read the works of the major Iranian scholar Ibn Sina, otherwise known as Avicenna, but says he is not convinced by his theory of earthquakes and the genesis of mountain formation. No, for his part, Nono can only see things being swallowed up, things collapsing. And he sticks to his opinion, even when people attempt to show him that by all logic, one must necessarily be the corollary of the other.

The epicenter of a given tremor, its number of victims, date, intensity, number of aftershocks, tsunamis, tidal waves, landslides, and other collateral damage have no further mysteries for him. All it takes is for someone to offhandedly name a city or country, and he instantly takes hold and begins reciting all that he knows about the geological phenomena that took place there, and how they interacted with the telluric activity in the area. He doesn't even need to consult the innumerable documents he has collected, photocopied, and stored away over the course of his research, making people wonder where he digs them all up. He has dedicated all his time, all his energy, and all his money to this.

ABOVE ALL, DON'T LOOK BACK

Inspired by the recent events that have stirred up his passion and exclusive interest in the history of the earth, his sole occupation is currently limited to drawing up lists. Various lists. Lists he revises and updates when he makes new discoveries. With categories organized in alphabetical, geographical, and chronological order, or else according to the intensity of tremors.

These days he is drawing up another, more painful, more difficult kind of list, where everything must be classified according to the official death tolls. As he keeps trying to get the exact numbers, his approach is incompatible with the tendency to generalize and approximate that characterizes all information concerning major catastrophes. His biggest problem is that they only talk about tens, hundreds, thousands, ten of thousands of victims—dead or missing. Give or take a few. The persistent repetition, unbearable for him, of the word "about" shows up systematically in every single survey. Thus, at Spitak, northern Armenia, December 7, 1988, one of the most violent tremors ever recorded on the planet Earth, we read: about 55,000 dead. Consulting these documents, he grows angry and begins to yell: but what in the world is this supposed to mean, about? About 55,000 dead or missing! Not 54,998 or 55,002! A life, two lives, ten lives, hundreds of lives—nothing! Nothing as far as they're concerned! A woman, a child, a mother, a spouse, a son—all nothing, nothing at all!

He punctuates his anger by shaking his fist at the sky, as if he were trying to make God witness the lack of respect survivors have shown toward the missing, or else to include him among the accused.

He has written to everyone who records statistics on natural catastrophes. To every head of state. He has contacted all the relevant authorities: institutes of history, geography, geodynamics; centers for the monitoring of movements in the earth's crust. He has sent messages to all the seismologists, geologists, volcanologists, oceanologists, and researchers the whole world over. Asking them to provide him with the exact numbers, right

ABOVE ALL, DON'T LOOK BACK

down to the last victim. The same basic letter, in French and English, and in Spanish for the South American countries, often affected by tremors and landslides.

For the moment, he hasn't received a single satisfactory answer. The president of the Republic of Turkey was the only one to reply, sending him a letter that requested he address himself to the relevant specialists and included a list of organizations that might be able to assist in his research. With his best regards.

Tonight, the big news that he just announced to anyone who happened to be listening was the following number he just discovered a few moments before while looking at an Internet site: 51.

Los Angeles, January 1994: 51 dead.

Fifty-one.

This is the rare detail that pleases him so much. It rekindles his belief in humanity. This one dead person more, this one dead person who was not rounded off in the count, no doubt because the total was not sufficiently deadly. Or maybe because in the United States and in developed countries the life of a man is clearly more precious than in a country like ours, discreetly referred to as a third-world country, and where we don't even bother to try to keep track of the precise number of violent deaths, whether they be by the force of nature or by the hands of man.

Khadija is a hairdresser. More than ten years ago, she opened a hair and beauty salon in a small, unpretentious site in the center of the 140-Unit Housing Project. She chose a name that a friend of hers had suggested and that she liked very much: "le jardin parfumé," the perfumed garden. Neither she nor her friend could have known that it was also the title of a treatise on erotology written in the nineteenth century by a Persian writer, a certain Sheikh Nefzaoui. A remarkably well-documented work filled with torrid eroticism. Some considered it pornographic. Once she realized her mistake, it was too late to get the sign changed. So she had to tolerate the gibes of certain well-read youths who were very familiar with this licentious work, available in the original and in translated versions in every bookstore in the capital. None of them have ever dared to reproach her about it openly, but more than once she has found the salon's window and sign splashed over with red paint.

Of course, all of this made her want to read the book in question. Whenever a well-informed client pointed out the unfortunate, scandalous connotations of the name, Khadija had learned to hurl it back at them: "Poetically speaking, has not a woman's hair always aroused men and fulfilled their desire? Has it not been, ever since time immemorial, the quintessential object of male fantasy? Really, there couldn't have been a luckier coincidence. Is it not for this very reason that hair has to be hidden from view?"

She has always held her ground, over these past years, despite the threats. Even going as far as to open a clandestine hair salon in her home when her activity was declared illicit by a group of young people from the housing project who were dressed in Afghan-style clothing, had beards, and looked slovenly, with lines of kohl drawn under their eyes.

Even when she felt the most overwhelmed by despair, she never stopped taking care of herself. Putting on her makeup, dying her hair (golden brown with ash blond highlights, she specifies), crimson nail polish, and long hair-removal sessions.

ABOVE ALL, DON'T LOOK BACK

These are the things that have made it possible for her to resist succumbing to the feeling of depression that is in the air, that slowly gnaws away at all women, continually subjected to the persecution of preachers, present in great numbers as if they had crawled out from the very depths of the shaken earth; a depression that completely robs them of their will to live, or rather to survive.

So it was Khadija alone, without the prompting of a psychologist or any other kind of soul doctor present in the neighborhood, who came up with the idea that would later transform the whole atmosphere of the camp; an initiative with highly therapeutic objectives and which could rightly be called revolutionary, destined to counteract the neurasthenic effect of the accusations against women: free hairstyling and beauty sessions for all women young and old who wanted them. *All* women, even those who were so terrorized by the idea that they could be accused of wanting to provoke more disorder or another catastrophe that they had renounced all forms of seduction.

Hair dryers, caps, rollers, clips, combs and brushes, color kits, conditioning creams, beauty products: all the necessary material had arrived by way of an association of women in Algiers, contacted with the utmost discretion.

Ammi Mohammed, the camp's chief, known as Multiservice Moh, a former herbalist who had switched to the grocery business and then to administration, was consulted for his knowledge of herbal medicine. He courteously supplied the plant and mineral-based natural products: henna, green clay, *ghassoul,** *messouak,*† kohl, and other ingredients. He had also taken it upon himself to regularly supply Khadija, and anyone else interested, with preparations that had been soaked for long hours and brought to them especially from the interior: ointments, balms, masks, and decoctions. All extremely efficient, as he guarantees.

*A type of clay used as a traditional beauty treatment for skin and hair. —TRANS.

† A tree whose twigs are rubbed on the teeth to clean and whiten them. —TRANS.

ABOVE ALL, DON'T LOOK BACK

And it is in this way that our afternoons began to vibrate with other tones, becoming more vivid, more colorful, rustling with daring and exquisite feminine secrets; and here and there more pervasive, more subtle, and above all more agreeable scents had begun to replace the pestilential odors of the latrines exacerbated by the heat.

Khadija seats her guests—she won't let anyone refer to them as clients—on a plastic chair in the middle of the tent where they are completely hidden from view. Water boils on the camp stove. There is a red plastic basin for clean water; a blue plastic basin for catching rinse water that will be used again. A rudimentary, makeshift installation that reflects the living conditions in the camp. This does not stop the women from coming in droves.

Khadija bustles around her guests. Full of consideration, she lifts their hair, estimating the type, length, and thickness, and then begins work. Armed with combs and scissors, she circles about them and, without asking questions, lets them explain how they see themselves and how they would like to be seen. Blond highlights, straight or curly hair, chignons, layered cuts, and lion's manes—she can do it all; the client needs only to express her desire. For color jobs and highlights, she has hired several girls who help and accept her directions and orders without complaint. She says she is teaching them the profession, and that this could be a good skill for them someday.

She starts to talk only when she senses that her client, who has come to be taken care of, to be touched gently, with respect, *needs* to be spoken to. She knows how to be discrete and listen when necessary. From time to time she slips a rai cassette into the stereo, and when a song she likes comes on, she raises the volume and breaks into a dance step in the middle of the tent, until one, two, and eventually a whole group of women gradually join in, accompanied by other guests who clap to the beat.

Every day, for hours on end, she cuts, pulls, curls, straightens, piles up, and lathers; and in her expert hands the most disobedient locks soften and become disciplined, the roughest, driest, most tired skin relaxes and firms up again. It is not unusual to see tears shine in the eyes of women and girls when they discover the result in the mirror.

At present, Khadija is a bit overworked, but she never turns anybody away. For beauty treatments, she gets help and advice from all those women who know about ancestral beauty secrets. Ancient knowledge is exchanged, and then the beautifying effect of a given secret is tested out on several guests and the results compared.

There are crowds of guests now. They even come from neighboring camps. Some wait for hours, seated all around the tent. Many bring tea, coffee, and little cakes with them; and in these moments spent together, some are even surprised to catch themselves laughing, letting themselves be swept along by a contagious desire to be happy.

It was one of these women, a particularly sharp-witted lady, who, one evening when she saw two thickly bearded men righteously turn their gaze and quicken their pace just as they passed by the group in front of Khadija's tent, called out loud and clear:

"Hey, Khadija! Don't you think you could have a go at men's hair from time to time? One afternoon a week, why not? You do hair removal don't you? And for free! You could also do shaving and washing . . . brainwashing . . . Let me tell you, you would be doing us all a huge favor!"

The woman looks at me intently. She is standing a few meters outside the entrance to the camp. She has been there for quite awhile it would seem. She is perfectly still. So still that she is almost rigid. With an excessively attentive and disturbingly unwavering quality to her gaze. Before I even notice that she is there, I feel the burning intensity of her gaze on me.

I look up. I set my book down on my knees. I straighten up. I stare back at her.

A bird flies overhead screeching, and the screech is like a streak across the sky.

She moves forward a step. Then another. She is wearing a dress made of bright blue fabric with large yellow flowers on it. It is a very long dress, with short sleeves, drawn tight at the waist with a silk cord. The kind of dress that is only worn at home or else under a djellaba. It is as though she went out without having taken the time to change. She has woven leather slippers on her feet. No scarf on her head. Medium-long hair, with red highlights in the sun, tinted with henna no doubt. As I study her face, she meets my gaze. She seems very tall from this distance, almost as tall as I am. She comes closer. She is close enough now for me to make out the twitching, or rather the trembling of one of her eyelids. A tremor that spreads over her entire face. She is no longer very young. About fifty or so perhaps. She reaches out toward me, grabs hold of my arm. Grips it strongly. I have the impression her fingers are going to leave a mark on my skin. I try to twist free. Her face tenses up suddenly into a wounded expression.

"Don't you recognize me?"

I don't know how to answer. My heart is beating so violently that I am having a hard time breathing. Is it possible that they have located me? But no—no I don't recognize her—I have never seen her before. Not a single sound escapes from my mouth. She repeats:

"Don't you recognize me?"

I close my eyes, gripped by an overwhelming sense of vertigo. Then I take hold of myself.

ABOVE ALL, DON'T LOOK BACK

This is no time to break down. I have to answer. I have to say to her right now, without panicking, without losing my grip, that I don't recognize her, that I can't recognize her because I have never met her before. Yes, I have to say that. Simple as can be. All that holds my life together now are long spans of emptiness and dark. I have to find shelter in denial. Ignorance. It is the only possible way out of this. I don't know. I have no idea.

Why, oh why, at this precise moment when I was paralyzed by her burning stare, did I feel something twist inside me, then turn over? Why did I feel thousands of little pricks all over my skin, as if I were suddenly overrun by thousands of tiny creatures clinging and climbing up my legs, quickly, so quickly, more and more quickly, using all their pincers? Do you really want me to go on?

"No I, I . . . I don't know."

She shakes me violently, as if to force me to listen to her, to answer her differently.

"Amina. Amina. *Benti,* my girl. Don't say that you don't recognize me. I couldn't bear that. Now that I've found you again, I wouldn't be able to . . . Don't say anything more now, whatever you do. I know how you must have suffered ever since . . . since . . ."

Dadda Aïcha is not around. It's Monday. And on Monday she goes to the hammam with Nadia. But the hammam is too far away for me to escape to; I can't just run there, find her, ask her to hide me, protect me, keep me. She won't be back until maybe one or two o'clock. And I can't bring myself to say to this woman that my name is not Amina, and that I have no idea why she is talking to me about some other girl named Amina. But it has to be done. I have to tell her. No. I am Wahida now. Ever since . . . since . . . I think I did know a girl named Amina once, but it was a long time ago, a very long time ago. I could tell her that, just to calm her down, to get her to look elsewhere. To make her go away and leave me alone.

ABOVE ALL, DON'T LOOK BACK

Once again I tell you, I repeat, that none of this has anything to do with me, it's all too complicated. I can't. May the earth open up again and swallow me whole. If only I didn't have to face all these staring eyes, these questions, these women, all these women . . . their frowning faces, their hands reaching out and coming toward me like snakes . . . and the odor. That odor again. Intense. Terrible. Swiftly exhumed. Like on the first day.

I have just realized that we are not alone anymore. Many women have come out of their tents. I didn't see them, didn't hear them coming. Without a sound, but also without hesitation, they are drawing close. They surround us. Khadija the hairdresser, Samia, Asma, and Khalti Kheïra are there among the other curious women who are close enough to be within earshot of what is said. Some of their kids are with them, holding onto their skirts. They have formed a circle around us and are drawing in gradually. You would almost say the group is slithering up in a reptilian manner. They seem to be still holding back a bit, but they're so interested in the conversation that they don't say a word. Apparently captivated by this turn of events. Waiting for even the slightest piece of gossip that could break the monotony of the camp routine.

I turn toward Khadija. The one closest to all of us. The one who knows us best. There must be some nervousness so apparent in my glance that she senses it and feels obliged to do something. She steps forward:

"Who are you, O woman?"

"Me? Dounya. My name is Dounya," answers the woman.

She goes over to her, takes her arm, repeats:

"I'm Dounya. I live over there, not very far away."

With her arm raised in the direction of the city, she points to an indefinite place that is, in any case, impossible to make out. We can't see a thing from where we are. The camp is located on the periphery of the city, on the margins of any life, pretty far away from any houses, in the same spot where the new housing projects were once being raised.

ABOVE ALL, DON'T LOOK BACK

Without moving, Khadija insists:

"Who are you? What are you looking for?"

"I already told you. My name is Dounya, and I'm looking for my daughter, for my daughter, Amina. She disappeared on the day of the earthquake."

She comes back toward me. She is so near that I can smell her scent, a mixture at once musky and acidic of perfume mixed with sweat. I have the sudden anguishing sensation of being a crazed animal, caught in a snare, surrounded by hostile staring eyes. I feel trapped by a beam of light so blinding it obscures and annihilates everything else. I can't understand what is happening to me. Having been through hell, I thought I was strong. I thought I was ready to hear anything, to endure anything. And especially, to face anything. Yet it is enough that this woman approach me, look at me, and speak to me for me to completely lose my grip, and my power over words, which remain cowering inside.

Unexpected and violent as the stab of a knife, an image flashes before my eyes of a little girl so terrified that although she wants to scream, no sound escapes from her mouth; a little girl in tears, overwhelmed by fear and pain, driven back against a wall by a man whose face, whose fists are threatening her. Where? When? I don't know. I'm not sure. Only the suffering and fear remain intact. And a terrible feeling of helplessness that, at this instant, sweeps away and annihilates all desire, all capacity to resist.

Khadija is speaking to me now: "Tell us, Wahida, do you know this woman? I mean . . . do you recognize her?"

I have the impression of being on trial for some crime. The faces I see around me are attentive, concentrated faces that seem to be waiting to judge and condemn me. All the same, I try to convince myself that there is nothing to be afraid of. That this woman is looking for her daughter. Lost, missing, gone forever, buried under tons of scrap metal or loose stone, or . . . I don't know. She came all the way here and believed she found her daughter in me. Why me? Is it possible that someone told her . . . ? It doesn't matter what they told her. All I have to do is deny

it, calmly deny it, looking her straight in the eye, like Amina
with the bus driver who drove her far away from home. All I
need to do is answer her with all the self-assuredness and calm
needed under such circumstances. Tell her straight out that I'm
sorry, that unfortunately she's following the wrong path, that
there's no doubt about it. All I need to do is to ask her politely—
not without an edge of exasperation in my voice—to please
admit that any resemblance that she sees to an existing, or formerly existing, person can only be the fruit of her imagination
gone astray. That my parents are dead. Declared dead, buried
for good, under tons of scrap metal and loose stone. That there,
in the tent, in a black leather case, wrapped in a plastic bag,
hidden between two blankets, blankets that are stacked on a
huge stone that serves as a shelf for our belongings, I even have
papers that can prove it. Very official documents saying that
Wahida really does exist.

As I am thinking all this over very quickly, other people
have come to join us and take in the spectacle. Here we are at
present in the middle of a crowd that keeps growing. This is
so typical. As soon as a stranger comes here, the news starts
flowing. You never know what might happen. Wouldn't want
to miss a significant event, or even an event that is important
enough to shake up the unfolding of the day a bit; especially
considering that nobody really comes to see us anymore, ever
since people here started getting fed up with the charade of
pretending that "everything's great" for the television cameras.
We are starting to have the reflexes of a real family now, united
for better and for worse. And especially for worse, considering
the situation.

"I don't know her. I've never seen her before."

It may be the presence of all the people around me that
has given me the strength to utter those words in a clear and
intelligible voice. I am relieved to hear, at the same time as I say
it, that my voice isn't trembling. Just the idea that everyone is
waiting for an answer is already enough to make me resolute,
so no one could possibly question my statement. My truth.

I turn to face her. I look her straight in the eye. She stares at me. Surely she has to realize now that she has made a mistake. In front of the whole group. Surely she has to agree to leave me alone. She has to stop trying to recognize something in me. Amina no longer exists. She has to come to terms with that. Even if it must be very painful for her. Even if she is sure that Amina is right there in front of her. She has to come to terms with it. She has to.

I step forward a bit more, almost touching her.

From this distance, she must feel my will—my willing her to leave, to go away, to calm down, to lower her eyes. A will so strong that I'm trembling. But instead of backing away, she seems to want this closeness. She stares at me. I don't lower my eyes. She still has that tremor which is now spreading in ever deeper, ever faster waves all over her face. She ends up stepping back slightly, as if disturbed by the defiance she can read in my eyes. Yes, that is what it is—she is disturbed. She passes her hand over her face and holds her forehead as if overcome by dizziness.

A bit of excitement, a ripple passes through the gathered crowd. There are noticeable reactions, yet I can't quite determine their nature. Approval or objection? Around here, who knows . . . ? Dadda Aïcha, or more likely Nadia, would they have . . . ? No, that's impossible. Impossible also to accuse Mourad. He almost never talks to other people. He is happy just to make himself useful, when he can, whenever someone asks him for help. He's not the type to go . . . and in any case, he was the one who got us the documents. The declarations of loss that have given me an official existence once again.

Slightly louder, so that everyone can hear, I repeat, looking her straight in the eye, addressing myself directly to her: "No. I don't know you."

I turn around, to indicate that for me the discussion is over. Before standing up, I put my book down on a stone, in front of the tent. I bend over to pick it up. Today I won't be getting any further in my reading.

Book in hand, I hesitate for a moment: whether to turn my back on them, go inside, and let down the curtain, or to get away until things return to normal. I wish that this spectacle would be over, that these women would return to their usual daily activities: cooking, laundry, gossip, television, and other pastimes. That the children would return to their playgrounds amid the dust and pebbles, and most of all that this woman with her strange ways would go away immediately. She has disrupted an afternoon that otherwise promised to be serene.

My indifference does not seem to have an impact on her determination. She has taken hold of herself. She steps forward, tramples right across my shadow, and grasps my arm once again. Facing the still hushed and attentive crowd, a crowd that she seems to want to bear witness, she declares in a voice that is weary and interrupted by sobs:

"I know, I know. I don't blame you. You can't remember. They told me it would be like this. But as God is my witness, I've already been walking for days and days, and it's toward you that my steps have led me. God has heard my prayers. I was at every hospital, every camp, I knocked at every door. I searched in every pile of ruins and heaved pieces of rubble aside. I asked everyone who passed by. I walked for miles and miles on end—by day as by night. I braved the sun, the dark, and the heat; fatigue, thirst, and hunger. From the peaks of mountains, I shouted into the wind, so that it would carry my calls along and spread them wide. I shouted out your name, hoping it would echo its way to you. And I knew, I just knew that I would find you one day. I knew I would be able to hold you in my arms once again. But who cares about the path that led me here, since here you are before my eyes, since here we are reunited once again. My girl, my little girl, fruit of my womb, my loved one, my love . . ."

Her voice breaks off. She looks as though she is about to faint. Khadija hurries over to her. She holds her up. But the woman has already taken hold of my arm. I have no choice but to steady her and help her sit down on a stone in front of the tent.

And the funny thing is—would you believe it?—against all odds, as incredible, as unexpected as it might seem, I realize

that her words have touched something inside me. Something
tucked away in a place that I thought was well out of reach.
I feel a little creature, dead to the world for a very long time,
begin to pulsate, to tremble again, and I can't stop it, I can't
halt this deeply interior agitation.

So I am seized by a violent emotion, shaken up by the force
and sincerity of the love song I heard just now. And I am not
the only one. Sniffles can be heard here and there, and when
I lift my head, my vision blurred by tears, I notice that all the
women present are drying their eyes with the backs of their
hands or the corners of their scarves. Like a wave that suddenly rises out of a seemingly flat sea, an emotion has overcome
all these women whom one might have expected hardened to
all suffering owing to the incalculable number of calamities
that have fallen on them over recent years. Every single one of
them. Some are even shaking with outright sobs they don't try
to hide. Others have let themselves fall into the arms of their
nearest neighbors and, closely entwined, hide their faces so that
others can't see them crying. Impressed by all this, the children,
who seem to have been affected by this tremendous swell, press
even closer to their mothers, out of fear of being swept away in
turn.

I'm not sure if it is Khadija who pushed me toward her, or
if I was the one who took her into my arms, from emotion and
compassion.

In the eyes of this woman, who is persuaded that she is
my mother, who is apparently deranged, apparently victim to a
passing confusion brought on by a recent traumatic event, like
so many other men and women in this place; in the eyes of this
poor soul, who at this very moment seems convinced that she
has finally found what she treasured most in the world, nothing
that I could subsequently say or do has been able to erase that
gesture.

The house is a bit on the outskirts of a residential area, facing a large vacant lot, at the very end of a road. It is barely visible from the exterior. Its surrounding wall, crumbling in places, is partially covered by a jumble of climbing plants—creepers tangled with ivy. Leaning over the door, sagging under the weight of its branches, an exuberant bougainvillea with dark red flowers seems to deliberately block the gate. It would appear that nobody has been through here for a long time.

As we walk along a pathway covered in gravel and leading to a building with decrepit walls, Dounya questions me. These are the first words she has addressed to me since we left the camp. She asks me if I am aware that the tenants of this house—our cousins who were driven away by terrorism—have been living in France for over ten years now. We have only been using the rooms that are on the first floor. The entire upper floor is empty and closed off, she adds.

I don't reply. She doesn't seem to expect an answer. I haven't said a single word during the entire taxi ride here.

Night has nearly fallen, and as we move slowly toward the front door, hundreds of birds sheltered in the thick foliage of the trees start making an appalling racket.

As I follow Dounya into a small entry hall, I am struck by the unexpected coolness of the house, which contrasts with the warmth of the night. We are greeted by the odor of stale air, and worse yet, a musty smell, which seems to have taken over the place. An odor that unquestionably suggests neglect. Undoubtedly ensconced for decades. I will continue to find it everywhere. Opening wardrobes, drawers, and cupboards, unfolding sheets, moving the smallest of objects, pulling curtains aside to open windows. I find it hard to believe that this house is inhabited at all or that Dounya actually lives here. She doesn't notice my incredulity. I don't say anything.

The two main rooms on the ground floor, which she shows me very rapidly, have high, very high ceilings. That's all I can make out in the faint light.

We reach the end of a dark hallway. Dounya takes a key out of her pocket. She opens a door. She turns on the light.

"This is your room."

So, I've arrived. She assures me that I am home.

It is a fairly small room. In the middle of the room, there is a large bed, covered with a cretonne bedspread that has a brown and orange design on it matching the double curtains on the window opposite the bed. On the right, a solid wood wardrobe with three doors, added molding, and a large beveled mirror in the center. Just opposite, near the door, a dressing table in the same style whose marble top is partially covered by a large crocheted lace doily, on which there are half-full bottles of perfume, apparently quite old, and many containers of every shape and size, made of wood, wicker, porcelain, and embossed leather. Obviously a collection. I open the drawers. In one of them, there are carefully folded sheets, adorned with ancient embroidery. In the other, there is an assortment of various colored towels. In the next, a number of tablecloths, also embroidered. Some still have their original tissue paper or cellophane packaging. In the last drawer, there are boxes containing brand-new underwear with their tags readily apparent.

Dounya is still behind me, standing in the doorway. She remains motionless as I inspect the room. I open the wardrobe. It is nearly empty. On two of the shelves, piles of linen or clothes have been covered over with a piece of white fabric, which is a small bedsheet perhaps. All the other shelves are empty. In the middle section, there is a rod. Suspended from clothes hangers are several pieces of clothing that are too small to be those of an adult. Yes, these must be children's clothes. A coat, a cardigan, two small velvet dresses in inverted colors: navy blue with a white collar and white with a navy blue collar. A little surprised, I turn toward Dounya. She has a strange expression on her face. Like a period of waiting tainted with anxiety, attenuated by a faint smile that attempts to cling to the corners of her lips. A smile that is nervous and undecided. You would say she was ready to burst into tears. Or perhaps, just as suddenly, just as irrationally, to burst into laughter. Once more I am filled with a flood of anxiety. I feel the uneasiness rising up in me, uneasiness that has taken over since I agreed to follow her all the way here and that has kept growing. If this is a game, then first of all I need to know the rules:

"It would seem . . . these are children's clothes. But if this is *my* room . . . then where are *my* clothes?"

I had a hard time thinking and saying the possessive pronouns aloud. But all the same, I managed to do it. As though I actually believed it. *My* clothes. *My* room. And here I have, by these very words, fallen headlong into the lie. These few words imply my acceptance. That I have agreed to let her believe she has convinced me. That I am going to enter into the story, despite all my reservations.

Up to now, all I did was obey and allow myself to be carried along by the course of events and perhaps also by the emotion and pressure I felt from all those who were present at this strange scene of a mother-daughter reunion. A sort of uncontrollable, irresistible euphoria.

And here I am, outlining the hypotheses once again—hypotheses that flow one into another, leading to this moment, to my presence in this house, faced with this woman I know nothing about.

As I follow her into the living room, the whole story reels through my head in reverse, like the sequences of a film rewinding.

If, by one of those chance occurrences nothing short of extraordinary, this woman hadn't met one of the two youths who had helped carry me over to Dadda Aïcha's tent, and who very precisely remembered the young girl who had lost her memory after being in shock,

if he hadn't been curious enough to stop and listen as she was telling her story to a group of people at the entrance of the local hospital,

if she hadn't gone over to talk to him and, impelled by a strange premonition, described to him the object of her quest in great detail, if he hadn't made the connection between the young girl that they had found passed out in the middle of the street and the story the woman had told him,

if, after putting me down in Dadda Aïcha's tent, he hadn't personally gone to look everywhere for a doctor to revive me,

if the doctor hadn't diagnosed me in front of him, proclaiming a case of posttraumatic amnesia,

if, being moved by the mother's despair, a mother who seemed so distraught and undone, he hadn't reconstituted the facts one by one,

if he hadn't shown her the exact location where I was living with Dadda Aïcha and where she could find me . . .

and above all, above all,

if, suddenly overcome by a desire to make a clean sweep of things, to start all over again, I hadn't voluntarily or involuntarily decided—I don't know, I'm not sure—to reinvent myself as someone else, to reinvent my life, my past, my name, my family . . .

All these stages of the quest . . . It was Dadda Aïcha who repeated them all to me before she let me go. She and Nadia had arrived at the very moment when the woman hugged me. After listening to Dounya tell the story in great detail of how she had found me, Dadda Aïcha asked me to go with her. I obeyed her willingly.

Dadda Aïcha recommended that I do one thing, one thing only, before taking me in her arms. "Now it is up to you alone to undo the knots that are inside you. You must find the end of the string."

I'm not too sure exactly what she was getting at.

Nadia, for her part, didn't want to hug me. She moved away and gave me a look that was so full of resentment that it was almost hostile, when I started to go over to her. At first I thought that it was because I was going to be leaving them, and so she felt abandoned. I was only able to grasp why she begrudged me so much when she forcefully pushed me away, turned her face the other way, and said: go on, go with your mother, leave us alone . . .

"These are your clothes. The ones you wore when you were little. The rest . . . they were over there, at your . . . with your aunt. We had taken everything there."

A mother. An aunt. Cousins. Far away, fortunately. As far away as this distance between us. On the other side of the Mediterranean.

The family is growing.

Who will be next?

Voilà, a new element is at hand. New characters are intervening in my story. I didn't think this would happen. At least not this way. It is my story, nobody else should be allowed to make use of it. I don't know how to play roles written by others. I have nothing prepared for this sort of development. I'm angry with myself and I have no one to blame but me. I gave in to an emotion that is incompatible with what has gotten me this far. I wanted, I want to move on, alone and free, without weighing myself down with unneeded attachments, without allowing myself to be guided by my feelings. What should I do now? Keep quiet? Should I ask questions? Should I go all the way to the end of this story—a story whose strings are starting to slip away from me, to multiply? Why not turn on my heel right now, leave this place, close the doors to this house with its very distinct atmosphere, which has been preserved from the intrusions of time and bears the imprint of a past so totally, so profoundly, so utterly foreign to me that it seems as though everything here is pushing me away?

All I see is hostility in these walls, which are marked by ancient, or are they more recent, cracks—I don't know—and splotched with large blotches of humidity; in this shining, bulging, outdated furniture; in these trinkets from another era; in this tiling which is cracked in places and coming apart; in the unstylish colors of these sofa cushions; in these frayed carpets and dusty curtains. It would seem that life ended abruptly here.

It looks as if history passed this house by, unable to cause the slightest stir in the air, the slightest turbulence, the slightest hint of change. Yes, what I see here, what I feel, is profound and worrisome; it is stagnation, a kind of atemporality. Time that is frozen. Yes, that's it. Enough to make your head swim.

And these children's clothes. Mine, she tells me.

I backtrack. The door to *my* bedroom has remained open. No, definitely nothing seems familiar to me. I recognize neither this woman, nor this house.

I approach Dounya, who hasn't stopped staring at me.

"Where is my aunt?"

"Your aunt? Dalila? May God bless her soul. No one was able to tell me . . . She was at home when the earthquake struck, and the building . . . like all the others . . . and you, you . . ."

Okay then. Exit the aunt. Having disappeared as soon as she appeared. And Dounya, no doubt obsessed with her quest to find me, doesn't seem to be particularly affected. And the cousins are too far away to be of any help. I need to ask for more detailed explanations. Later. To know who I really am and what I am doing here. I don't feel like going any further today. Everything ends up getting muddled in my head. Tired. I am tired. Too many emotions. And above all, too late to go back. For the moment, I feel like sleeping. Here where I am. In this room that is mine, she says. In this bed that is mine as well.

She attempts to lead me toward the kitchen. I turn away. No, really, I don't want to eat, no, I'm not hungry at all, please don't insist. Tomorrow. Let's see tomorrow.

Once she has left, I close the door. The bed is made. Enveloped in the smell of the house that is so inhospitable, I slip between the sheets without getting undressed. I came empty-handed. I left the camp as destitute as when I arrived there. I have just enough time to think that I'm cold, very cold, after the furnacelike conditions that reigned in the tents both day and night, and that I ended up getting used to, just enough time to think about the rediscovered comfort of a real bed and a real mattress, to realize that, oddly enough, at this very moment, I feel absolutely no apprehension, and I fall asleep.

Reprinted in a number of newspapers, many days in a row—the notice is very precise. It is easy to spot inside a box in the center of the page. And in contrast to the majority of the missing persons notices that have been filling the inside pages of daily newspapers ever since the catastrophe struck, this one does not include a photograph. The description, however, is very detailed: "I am looking for my daughter, first name Amina. Age: 23. Tall, approx. 170 cm. Very slender. Long black curly hair. Light brown eyes. Thin eyebrows. Pale complexion. Distinguishing mark: a dimple on her chin."

Other than the distinctive characteristic mentioned, this portrait could be that of thousands of other girls. Except it happens that I am 169 cm tall, and that I do have an easily distinguished cleft in the middle of my chin.

The rest of the notice includes details concerning the location and circumstances surrounding the disappearance. "When the earthquake struck, she was at her aunt's house in the 80-Unit Housing Project, building 4, fourth floor. Certain people have confirmed that they saw her afterward in a number of places in the city. Any person who has seen her or is able to provide information of any sort is asked to please contact Madame B. Dounya at 20 Rue du 20 Août, formerly Rue des Glycines."

As I read, something occurs to me which is absurd and incongruous at this moment: a great many neighborhoods, streets, squares, and stadiums—recently built or else renamed—are now known simply as a number, a simple figure meant to help the population memorize the utmost facts of our history. Nothing reassures members of our government more than numbers and dates, commemorations and historical references, more specifically, references to the revolutionary past of the country, which many of them draw on these days, seeking a form of legitimacy that is increasingly contested. A revealing toponymy. As good a way as any to keep accounts when you fail to repay the balance.

Dounya got out all the newspapers for me and spread them open on the kitchen table. She was up early, very early. I heard

ABOVE ALL, DON'T LOOK BACK

her. I fell back asleep very quickly. Before making coffee, she has waited for me to get up too. As soon as I sit down, without asking me anything, she serves my breakfast. A cup of black coffee and, on the side, a large glass of hot, very hot milk with only a touch of sugar in it. I never drink café au lait. I draw near the table, and it is while I am blowing on the hot milk before taking a sip, which is what I always do, that I realize that she has served me without asking what I want. And it is exactly what I always have every morning. I look at her. Her back is to me and she is busy at the sink. I choke back the question I'm dying to ask.

When I opened my eyes this morning, it took me a few minutes to reassemble all the scattered elements of my story, just as it does every day. To realize that I am no longer at the camp. That I am in a house I am supposed to know or recognize somehow. I am really here. In this room. In this bed with its flowery sheets. With a woman who is holding on to me with every ounce of her strength. A woman who offers me a history, a past, a refuge, and the kind of love that cannot be put in doubt. There is also something else, an indefinable feeling linked to the atmosphere of this house, to the closed doors, to the mysteries that I infer, to the objects which now, in the light of day, seem to have taken on a whole other allure, a sort of life of their own, as though detached from their external environment which has allotted them no space whatsoever.

Particularly restless, Dounya radiates around me. She moves a chair. Sits for a few seconds. Then stands back up again. She opens her mouth as though to say something or make an observation, snaps it shut without saying anything, sits back down again, pours herself more coffee, moves toward the open window, seems to lose herself in contemplation of the garden for a long drawn-out moment, before finally coming back toward me.

I have the impression that she is waiting for something. A word. A gesture. Questions perhaps. Reflections concerning what I think about her, about me, about us, about this first night spent together under the same roof. About the house, finally rediscovered. About what happened to me before. During the interval of time in which, according to her, we lived apart. Yes, she is waiting, there is no doubt about it. I can see it in the way she is standing, slightly stooped with her shoulders slumped, her head slightly tilted to one side. There is also that way she has of breathing very quickly when she is troubled by a worrisome thought, of sighing from time to time, of striving not to allow anything to show on her face, no feelings whatsoever, of always trying to appear on guard, of observing me out of the corner of her eye, and of never holding my gaze for more than a few seconds. Everything about her body indicates that she has never known how, or managed, to relax completely. As if held back by some immemorial sense of modesty or perhaps some immemorial pain.

And so *my* declared or supposed mother hesitantly begins . . . and since you don't know, since you don't know anymore, I must start by telling you that we had not been living together for some time. You must have noticed this when you came in and saw your room again.

Let me explain.

Maybe something in what I'm going to tell you will help you to recall what it is that you were. What you were for me. Why weren't we living together anymore? Quite simply because your aunt agreed to take you into her household during the whole time that I was . . . that I was sick. Because right after your father passed away, I became ill. Seriously ill. For a very long time. They had to hospitalize me. You wouldn't remember that, you were too young. Fortunately. But don't worry, everything is fine now. I am better, much better . . . and since I managed to find you, nothing else can happen to me. You have always lived with me, within me, even when we were separated. Do you need me to tell you that? You are my daughter and my only child. You never knew your father. I don't know what that might mean to you. It doesn't matter. I have you now. Your grandmother is dead, she died a long time ago, just after your father. That is why I had no choice but to entrust you to your aunt Dalila, my sister. May God bless her soul and welcome her into his great paradise! And she was forced to work in order to meet our needs. Before that, we lived here. You and I. In this house. And then when I, when I fell ill, it was our cousins who took over the house for many years. When they left, they took most of the furniture with them. That is why the house seems so empty to you, almost as though it were abandoned. And there was nothing that I could do about it. Those cousins are all the family that we have left now. But I already told you all of this, don't you remember?

But tell me, what about you, even if . . . even if you were very little, don't you remember anything? No memory of the hours and days that we spent together? Yes, I know, I know it all too well, you were too little to be affected by . . . to be af-

ABOVE ALL, DON'T LOOK BACK

fected by what we were to each other. But I have a hard time believing that my face, my arms, and my love have left absolutely no mark on you and that you can't remember your own mother.

Her voice becomes vehement, accusatory.

We are seated in armchairs in the living room. Face-to-face. I can't make out her features or the expression on her face. I can only see her silhouette, haloed in light, lit from the back. Because I was depressed by the dim light, I opened all the windows and threw the shutters back before I sat down. Now a ray of sunlight is playing upon my dress. It crawls onto my knees. Its warmth goes right through the fabric. It spreads to my stomach. Everything else is cold, frozen. But I feel fine. I have no desire to move. No desire to answer her. I know she doesn't expect an answer.

She is quiet for a moment. Then continues. More softly. More tenderly. Swept along by memories that erase all resentment. A lament or a litany, I don't know. The sentences come out, wave upon wave, one after another, and reach these shores where I am.

"For a long time, a very long time after I brought you into this world, I still kept the mystery of your presence imprinted inside the hollow warmth of me, moist and moving, and the weight of your body, the enigma, flutter, sound, and beating of your heart, like some fragile little bird held captive in the innermost part of my being. I recall your first smile, which was for me alone; your first smile, imprinted in me forever. I recall the sound of your voice when you said mama for the first time; its tender clear timber, engraved in my memory forever. And the first bubbly notes of your laughter—I have gathered them all and preserved them together preciously. For the longest time, I was refreshed by the way your face lit up when I took you in my arms. And my hands, these very hands, as you can see, have kept the memory intact, indelible, and wonderful, even today, of the smoothness and warmth of your skin.

"Do you know that even today, from a thousand smells

smell - 1ˢᵗ sense you remember as a child. A sign of rebirth, return to primitive self

122

ABOVE ALL, DON'T LOOK BACK

and with my eyes closed, I could still recognize that scent of milk that I inhaled around your neck, a scent of childhood and innocence, bitter and delicious at the same time?

"One at a time, I have kept as an offering each word you learned and brought to me, with wobbly steps.

"I picked you up when you fell and I blew on all your wounds.

"I carried you.

"I rocked you night after night, and for you, in a whispery murmur I would sing just as one breathes, one caresses, one clasps something dear.

"I watched over you on nights when your dreams were so haunted by monsters and disappointments that you couldn't sleep, and with just my voice I chased away the darkness and swept away your fears.

"I dried your tears and I comforted you when you cried.

"I celebrated all of your birthdays, even when you weren't there, with paper flowers and with candles I kept lit all night long in the heart of my solitude, until they burned down. I would have liked to be by your side, but I couldn't be.

"A little later on, I would have liked to teach you myself all about the sky and the clouds, the night and the stars, the earth and the seasons, and the colors of the sea. But I wasn't able to do it.

"Like a shadow fastened to your footsteps, I followed you everywhere, to all the places where you would go, without you knowing it, and I never imagined, for even one day, not even one moment, that I might never see you again.

"I would have liked to share in your astonishment, your discoveries, hear your giggles, rejoice in your happiness, hush your complaints, and protect you from the dark. But I wasn't able to.

"But you must, you must understand. All that kept me going was knowing that you were still alive, still present, even if far away from me.

"The only times I was happy was when, for a few fleeting moments, I closed my eyes and saw you running toward me.

ABOVE ALL, DON'T LOOK BACK

"And above all, above all, the only reason I stayed alive until today is to be able to hold you in my arms."

Eyes half-closed, arms folded over her chest, she rocks back and forth, as if to pacify or contain some unspeakable pain. She must not even be aware of this movement which gives her words a rhythm, a force of attraction that is almost impossible to bear. Out of breath and exhausted, she stops talking. But, as though she were carried along by some unbroken momentum, she continues rocking back and forth.

Now she is staring at me, but I know she doesn't see me. She is off somewhere. Her words, mixed with light that becomes brighter as she speaks, continue to resonate in the room. For a long time they remain suspended, before finally slipping outdoors and disappearing.

When she leaves the living room, I don't follow her. I try with all my strength to subdue the trembling that shakes me to the bone, as though I were suddenly numbed by cold or pain, while at the same time I try unsuccessfully to stifle the flood of emotion that has gripped me as she was uttering her incantation.

This woman is only a stranger to me—I want, have to believe it very strongly so that I won't lose my grip—this mother wants to convince me of her sincerity. She wants to reach me, to move me in turn.

Something stronger, more mysterious, further away and perhaps also more painful than love inhabits this woman. No doubt about it. But maybe there can't be love without suffering. I don't know. I'm not sure.

Very thin, very tall, with everything about her angular, even sharp-angled, Dounya does not exactly correspond to the image one might have of a mother, of a dignified and respectable housewife. Like those women whose only perfume is that of the household disinfectant or air freshener, women who are only able to recognize themselves when they can see their reflection sparkling at the bottom of a carefully scoured pot, women who store their illusions and dreams between two cans in a kitchen cupboard.

Flurries of images come back to me. Sometimes crystal clear, in surprisingly precise detail, other times blurry and muddled by obstructions that hinder any possibility of reconstitution. A sort of fluctuation in which characters, words, screams, landscapes, and places intersect.

Constant comparisons that I can't help making throughout the first days of our living together. Sometimes it happens that, for a very brief moment, fragments are superimposed, and I have a hard time matching the pieces, a hard time settling back into that particular reality. I still haven't gotten used to the idea that all the various factors have come together in such a way that I can now settle into the following certainties for a long time: I have a house; a room; a mother; a past; a scattered family of sorts, some of its members dead, some alive; and a lot of problems to solve, questions to ask that I'm not asking. That I don't want to ask. Why? I don't know. I'm not sure.

I am living at present in *my* room.

The household linens folded in the drawers of the dressing table are meant for *my* trousseau. A portion of it anyway. The other part to be provided, according to popular tradition, by my future suitor. It is a trousseau that reveals a distinctive taste for old things, collected piece by piece over many years by a farsighted mother. Which is perhaps what explains the faded, almost yellowing quality of the sheets and tablecloths. The almost new children's clothes hanging in the wardrobe were once *my* clothes. And as she shows me velour dresses and small wool coats, there is a little smile on her face to explain that she kept them so that I would be able to dress my own children in them. When I might have children of my own. When she would be a grandmother. They're all in good shape, she adds, but a bit too weakly, as though she were trying to justify herself. Besides, she continues, many mothers are never able to free themselves of the childhood image of their offspring, even when their son or daughter is well into their adult years. That's not too bad, is it?

I don't respond, since I am a little annoyed with the way she is prying and showing this almost obsessive attachment to everything to do with childhood—with *my* childhood.

All the clothes that I have been wearing since I got here belong or belonged to the previous inhabitants of this house, to one of the daughters perhaps. Dounya gave them to me. She found them, folded inside a suitcase, inside a closet. Clothes that are completely out of fashion, but exactly my size. Everything that *I owned,* she told me, was at my late aunt's house. All *my* belongings. They all disappeared along with her. I would need new identification papers, new proof of my official existence. Once again. But there was more that I would need to know too. When I am ready.

She explains things to me. In random bits. She provides me with the pieces to a puzzle which don't quite fit together. Some pieces are missing. And others clash with the whole. Dissonant notes. Contradictory. What did I do before? Nothing. No, *I* didn't have a job. No, *I* wasn't engaged. Yes, *I* did complete my lycée baccalauréat; *I* was a good student, but *I* wasn't able to go any further. Because . . . because of *my* mother's illness, of course. *My* aunt Dalila was very strict; she didn't want to let *me* go out. She didn't think it was a good idea that *I* should work either; taking a young girl into your home is a major responsibility. Of course, of course. I keep finding these words everywhere. These sentences. Uttered so many times. Heard so many times. Yes, that's right, *I* didn't work, but *I* could manage the entire household without the slightest difficulty. Which

ABOVE ALL, DON'T LOOK BACK

was, by the way, one of the reasons why *my* aunt held me in such high esteem. Excellent cook, yes, no one could equal *my* skills when it came to traditional cuisine: couscous, *chorba,** *bourek,†* *rechta,‡* and of course all sorts of sweets. Essential when you want to move up or get promoted from the rank of unmarried to married woman! Add to all this the most laudatory adjectives: polite, attentive, never a word spoken louder than another, cheerful, sympathetic, loving, charitable . . . the list goes on and on. *"A specialization at the tip of each finger,"* as Dadda Aïcha would say. All the ingredients you need to be in the running for the title of ideal daughter and wife, the sort who only exists in the dreams of a mother or else the always disappointed ambitions of a future mother-in-law. How surprising to have all this going for you and not already be tied down! No, no, *I* didn't wear a headscarf. Not yet. A well-behaved girl, *I* always said that *I* would obey my husband's wishes. Of course, of course. This too I know all too well. Every girl must get used to the idea that she will have to submit to her husband's desires. Don't forget the plural form. That's essential. Their desires. And the headscarf is part of those desires. Shielding one's wife, sister, or daughter from the eyes of others has become an unavoidable obligation, even an obsession for many men today. Just like the haik, worn by all women during the already distant colonial era on those rare occasions when they were authorized to leave their homes, which had the function of shielding them from the gazes and concupiscence of foreigners. You have to know how to preserve yourself entirely for the Elect by not stimulating easily excitable desires; this is how a virtuous girl and wife is recognized. And as far as I know, these days it is the girls themselves who are the most convinced of it.

---

* Special soup containing meat, vegetables, and grains, served especially during the month of Ramadan. —TRANS.

† Paper-thin pastries filled with meat, egg, parsley, etc. They are often served as an accompaniment to *chorba.* —TRANS.

‡ Noodles. —TRANS.

ABOVE ALL, DON'T LOOK BACK

"And . . . what about *my* pictures? Where are all the pictures? There must certainly be some. I would like to see myself again; it could help me to . . . to find myself, to find you again. You must have taken some, pictures I mean, as all mothers do. During all that time when you weren't sick . . . during all that time when we lived together . . . Me as a baby, a charming little girl, a bit chubby perhaps, me as a child, in my mother's arms or playing in the garden, me as an adolescent, sullen or fun-loving, posing or else refusing to look at the camera, me on the day of . . . What? Me, the child who was so loved, so present, and so dear was never, ever captured in a photo?"

As though she had been caught out, Dounya hesitates a brief moment. Her gaze becomes evasive, and her voice stumbles uncertainly over words.

"But I did, I did of course . . . I had tens of dozens of photos of you. Entire albums of you. But everything disappeared. Everything was at your aunt's house. I already explained that to you."

I believe I already mentioned that I don't believe in coincidences. Especially when they seem, how shall I put it, a bit too flagrant. Those that fit perfectly, in exactly the right way, at precisely the right moment, giving them a stronger resemblance to the common alibi or even the categorical lie than to the fruit of mere chance.

Apart from the clothes, I see nothing in this house suggesting the presence of a child or an adolescent. No toy, no book, no trace whatsoever of *my* past existence. No notebooks, no letters, no novels, no little scraps of paper on which there should have been a few scribbled lines of *my* life and *my* works, whether written or drawn, legible or incomprehensible. Nothing of the sort.

Here is something that ever so slightly sways the too beautiful building that has been patiently constructed and amiably described by the very woman who would like more than anything for me to call her mother.

Ever since I have been in this house, with no sense of urgency or even of time, I have had the almost physical sensation of letting myself slide down a slope, smoothly and without pain. Without desire and impatience either. As though I were contaminated by the sluggish atmosphere of this place. I don't know where it is taking me, nor when I will arrive. Everything seems tinged with unreality.

For the moment, I don't feel like digging deeper and bringing to light more of the darkness that I sense goes very deep. I have no desire to know what is hidden behind the closed doors, behind Dounya's silences, behind Dounya's weakness and her moments of reticence as soon as I ask a specific question about her life and her illness, about the reasons for and the length of our separation, about the conditions in which *I* lived when I was with her sister who had taken *me* in. She always finds an escape, a way to avoid my questions, reinforcing the feeling that I have of moving in a thicker and thicker fog, without a single point of reference.

For her part, she is happy just to watch me come and go in the house. I never hear her walking around, but I can sense her presence. She is never very far away from me. In the morning, when I wake up, the door that I closed the night before is ajar. So I end up leaving it wide open. I suppose she must worry that I'll leave. Sometimes when she doesn't realize that I am observing her, she has such eagerness in her eyes that I am a little afraid of her. Or else, as she comes toward me, I have the very distinct impression that she is moved by an irresistible impulse, a desire to touch me, to hold me in her arms. When I turn around, I discover her hand hovering above my head, as if about to stroke my hair. She senses my evasiveness, the instinctive way I jerk out of reach as soon as her hand rests on me. She never insists. We haven't yet reached out and hugged each other.

She goes out every morning. She does the shopping. Then she returns quickly. She doesn't work. I don't know where she gets the money she spends. I could ask her about it. But I do nothing of the kind. She prepares meals herself without ever asking me for help. Very light meals that she supplements with fruit and light, ready-made desserts. I could help her. But I don't. From time to time, she tidies up downstairs. Her house-keeping is very succinct. She rarely mops the floor and only in the kitchen. A few quick sweeps of the broom and a dust rag passed lightly over the furniture in the common area that we use as a living room. A very minimal arrangement: two sofas facing a television set, a very low armchair and a little table, all lost in an immense space. No rug, no knickknacks, no paint-ings on the walls. Things are intentionally stripped down to the basics, in total opposition to the usual thirst for accumulation and the shining clutter of living rooms, which is so characteris-tic of all houses I have known in the past, even the most modest ones.

I have never ventured into her room. She closes the door when coming out. I have never been curious enough to see what is inside, not even when she goes out. I don't know if she locks it with a key. If she takes the key with her when she leaves. She never goes up to the second floor. Or at least I have never caught her up there. One evening, I asked her if we could go in and just have a look. She avoided the question. Later, later, the rooms are almost empty in any case, there really isn't anything interesting except for a few pieces of furniture and some per-sonal belongings of the old inhabitants, our cousins. Nothing much really . . .

No one ever comes to visit her. The telephone placed on a little shelf near the entrance never rings. It would seem she doesn't know anyone. As if my presence alone fulfills her and has led her, ever since we started living together, to otherwise isolate herself.

She must realize that it intrigues me. I have nothing to do all day long other than go from my room to the kitchen, from the kitchen to the living room to watch TV, from the living room to the garden to take a little stroll, and from the garden back to the house. I don't even try to make myself useful, and this doesn't bother her. She herself spends the greater part of her time in her bedroom. I don't know how she passes those long hours in which she doesn't emerge.

We both sink into silence. A silence which is in tune with the very odd atmosphere of the house.

She will only say to me from time to time: you are all I have. I have no one other than you. And it is perhaps these words, these words alone which give me the feeling that I actually do exist, that I'm not just a bramble bush being tossed about by the winds—yes, these words alone keep me at her side.

Perhaps the earthquake has bumped us all into another dimension. Into another relationship with time and the reality of objects.

Perhaps all that has been happening since—all these visions, these encounters, these departures, these howls of revolt, and these threatening predications—are only vain attempts to put back together a world forever annihilated. Maybe we, the survivors who escaped, the disaster victims, the ones who have lived through this end of the world owing to obscure, inexplicable circumstances, have—without even realizing it—substituted another order for chaos, another equilibrium upon which time no longer has a hold.

Perhaps also the successive lies upon which I attempt to build my life are really only successive predetermined shifts toward another form of annihilation.

Thus, the dizzy spells and vertigo would be merely tangible manifestations of the effects of this slow suctioning in toward a hypogene world where nothing in the way of human construction and creation, whether material or spiritual, would be able to survive.

Dadda Aïcha sent Mourad to find me. We hadn't seen each other since I left. She simply wanted to hear my news.

He had no difficulty finding me. The pathetic story of a girl who was found many weeks after the catastrophe by a courageous and tearful mother had made its way around the region. No doubt around the whole world too, thanks to all the media covering the story. Fortunately, no photographers had been present to immortalize the moment. I too had read the article that pertained to us. A very detailed article, spanning many columns. With a special note, since for once, as the author stressed, "a faint glimmer of hope shines amid the terrible catastrophe that has once again struck the Algerian people whose resilience no longer needs demonstration"—there is a happy ending.

Both mother and child are doing well.

This article, entitled "At Long Last: Heartwarming Tales of Reunification," included numerous statements from Camp 8 disaster victims, and when it was published, another story was also dug up—that of a little girl who had disappeared during an earthquake that ravaged the city once known as El Asnam,* but since renamed Chleff, no doubt in order to ward off its bitter fate. The journalists who revived the story of the little girl, no doubt at the urging of the mother, seized the opportunity to call for witnesses more than twenty years after the fact.

But who would heed the call?

The man, a military officer by profession, who on October 10, 1980, a few minutes after the second tremor, even more deadly than the first, pulled up Nawal—the little girl who was three years old and suffered mild injuries to her knees—from the arms of her uncle who had just saved her life?

The individual or individuals who evacuated her by helicopter, taking her to a location where she would remain lost,

---

* Means "the idols" in Arabic, and these, as we know, were prohibited as objects of worship from the moment Islam appeared. Their destruction was one of the founding acts of the religion. Could there be a connection between these facts and the numerous earthquakes that have shaken the city (1954, 1957, 1980) . . . who knows?

despite the relentless quest of her mother, who spent many years crisscrossing the entire country, combing through every hospital, orphanage, and even every morgue without finding the slightest trace of her?

The family who took her in—a little girl now a fully grown woman—without knowing or in perfect knowledge of the facts, who can really say?

Or the young woman herself, intrigued by the title and content of the article and the details developed therein, or simply pushed into action by a mysterious premonition?

Dounya read the article before I did. She is the one who buys our newspapers whenever she goes shopping. She showed it to me. She asked me to read it. And on that day, she also started talking. In a flat tone of voice, she asked if I could understand the pain of a mother whose child, whose little girl, has been wrenched away from her. The pain she feels knowing that she is alive somewhere, far away from her. Then she left the kitchen. She went to the garden. She stayed there for a long time. Alone.

She was the one who opened the door when Mourad appeared at the gate.

Mourad, my little brother, here before me now, transformed, grown up, I could almost swear it, so sure of himself, so talkative, so pleased to announce to me his upcoming departure. To reassure me in a new tone, at once calm and serious, that he will send me news as soon as he arrives over there. That he will keep me up to date about everything. So happy to list for me all the steps he has had to take in order to finally be able to say with certainty that he will be reaching his goal. To describe for me in the finest detail all the various jobs he has had to do in order to raise enough money, and then give the required sum to an intermediary who will pay off the two sailors who have agreed to help him clandestinely embark on a boat destined for Europe. Which country exactly? He doesn't know. It's not important to him. Europe is immense; there's room for everyone who wants to succeed. He'll be a magician. People are fond of magicians over there. He knows the names and the tricks of the most famous magicians. He's seen them on television, wearing suits of lights. They are admired. They are acclaimed. They are respected. People make room for them. Even when they didn't get there by way of school. All they need is talent. And then, after that, Canada. Or Australia. The world is immense. It's just a matter of getting out of this country and then . . . He holds his arms wide open, as if to grasp the entire earth.

I am taken aback by the amount he declares as the price of a clandestine crossing. Yes, it is a considerable sum, yes, yes of course it is, but the result will also be considerable. The realization of all the dreams he has carried with him in his head for such a long time.

"But tell me, little brother, if I wanted . . . if I also . . ."

Mourad bursts into laughter. With a circular gesture, he indicates all there is around us. The house. The garden.

"You? For the moment, you are here, and you have all this. All this. And besides . . . besides, your mother . . . you wouldn't want to leave her now that she has found you! Hold on. But don't worry. Wait a while. Give me the time to get over there, to settle in . . . Then I'll find you someone there. Someone from here, of course. Someone who is good. Rich and all . . . And he'll come all the way here to get you. I won't forget you. I promise you that, Wahida. Oh, that's right! I forgot! You aren't called Wahida anymore! So, tell me, what are we supposed to call you now?"

When it is time to leave, he stands, facing me, and hesitates for a moment. I am the one to move toward him. I feel like kissing him on either cheek. He comes a little closer. Without looking at me, in an abrupt gesture, he leans his cheek toward me, then moves away very quickly. Like people without the habit of kissing, or of being kissed. Then he turns around and leaves, taking big, rapid strides.

Dullness, heaviness, idleness, and silence. One would say that since I have been here, I must have ingested a substantial dose of tranquilizers or something even stronger, some drugs with such powerful, long-lasting effects that they annihilate all desire in me, all will to move forward.

A strange tête-à-tête.

Days spent spying on each other, crossing each other's paths, observing each other like two boxers called into the ring who delay the moment of confrontation—each fighter waiting until he has identified his opponent's weak point.

One after another, the days dissolve, leaving in their wake only an oppressive faint impression of emptiness. We are living in trying suspense since there is nothing, no goal we are waiting for. As though we irrationally intuit the imminence of a terrible catastrophe. Even more terrible than the one that has brought us together.

And when the questions overshadow me in dense clouds, when they fill my head with their racket, their impatience—the odor starts spreading again. It's as if it were coming right out of me. Always so strong. Intense. Terrible. It even invades areas that I thought were protected until then. It spreads, as if to make me go back, to turn me back around. I push forward. Resist. With all my force. I don't want to give in. Clouds. Clearing. I close my eyes. I lock all the exits.

No, this whole thing can't last. We both know it very well. Behind us, a gulf at the bottom of which swarm silences and lies. In front of us, a space veiled in fog so thick that it's impenetrable and we can't even measure its extent. For the moment, we are standing on the same ledge, very close to one another, putting off, by tacit accord, the moment when we will have to resolve to move forward, both likely held back by the fear that all will be turned upside down again, one more time.

There are also signs. The ones we interpret. Always wanting to match them with answers that we hope to find. Also those we don't want to see and push aside; knowing, however, that we won't be able to ignore them forever.

I could open the doors and be on my way. Nothing could be easier. I know where the keys are. Dounya doesn't bother to hide them. First of all because she must realize that if I really wanted to, I would just leave. It is not closed doors that keep me here.

I could go back there, to the camp. Perhaps have a little space of my own in Dadda Aïcha's house, since she lives in a cottage now, like nearly all the earthquake victims. I know that she would be happy to see me, to take me in again and keep me close by her side.

I could also leave and go to some other place. But I know I can't do that today. Something is holding me here, in this house with its persistent strong odor despite all the living fragrances of life that blend with it—an odor that has now become familiar.

I get up in the morning, almost always at the same time. Always after Dounya. I know she doesn't sleep very much. I hear her walking around in her room a good part of the night. I go to join her in the kitchen. I know she is waiting for me. Her presence is no longer exasperating or difficult for me to bear. The house isn't either. Sometimes I even have the impression of an almost irresistible attraction. I don't know when and how it was born and developed in me. It seems to come from beyond my own consciousness. I don't know everything. I haven't yet discovered everything about that life, the one she is offering me. Sometimes I try to decipher what is hidden behind her brow, where two deep horizontal wrinkles are always visible and seem to furrow in even deeper when she looks at me. I try to surprise her, to wait until she is caught off guard and therefore more vulnerable before I sit down next to her and ask her a question. In the evening, for example, when we are sitting in front of the television. Any pretext whatsoever will do, for example a line picked up in passing from a film or a debate. But she refuses to talk about herself and revisit a past that troubles her so much that even the slightest mention of it puts her in a state of uncontrollable agitation. She doesn't want to venture beyond what binds us together, she and I, beyond this passion nourished by absence and deprivation. Everything in her is entirely, helplessly, and exclusively founded on the bonds that connect her to her child. It would seem that she exists today and has always existed solely as a mother, to judge by her reactions and sentiments. The allusions that I make, the detours and deviations that I follow in order to get a little closer to her, to raise the veil she has pulled down over a secret which I sense is there without being able to determine the nature, the seriousness, or the object—in a word, all my attempts to try to breach her defenses are in vain and come up against impenetrable resistance.

I decide to visit Dadda Aïcha and Nadia. Dounya comes with me. In the taxi that takes us to the camp, I try to recall the first trip I took with her. Everything is blurry. Confused. I have the sensation that ever since that day, I have been living in a dream, in an enclosed space, surrounded by closed doors whose keys I can't find.

When we arrive, I don't recognize the place. Where blue and green canvas tents once stood, I now discover a group of little houses, and this new development almost seems like a vacation colony.

Rectilinear lanes are bordered on either side by cottages, prefabricated, of course, but representing more comfort than anyone would have dreamed of even a few weeks ago. Slightly elevated in relation to the ground, and accessible by way of two steps, each chalet has two very small rooms inside, but there are windows, a door, walls, a parquet floor, and a ceiling. Everything made of wood. A real house in fact! There is even a little kitchen and a bathroom. Fairly rudimentary in its equipment, but still a considerable move up, even a real luxury for those who have lived with the lack of privacy and the foul smell of cesspools.

But the most important thing is feeling assured that no matter how strong the aftershocks may be, you can always escape . . . so long as the earth doesn't open up and swallow us all whole, adds Dadda Aïcha, who greets us on the doorstep. She is alone. Nadia hasn't got back from school yet. I thought I would find *my* grandmother cheerful and happy to have a roof over her head as she had so ardently hoped, but instead I find an old lady who seems a mere reduction of her former self, and she confesses to me that she is worried about Mourad, since she hasn't heard from him at all since he left. I find her to be shockingly transformed in such a short period of time. Less lively, less combative, older: abruptly overcome by age or perhaps worn down in some completely different way. The glimmer that infused her gaze with brightness and sharpness so rare in people of her age seems to have misted over, as if she were overcome by sadness, which she tries her best to hide from us at first. She still has Nadia by her side—her little girl, her miracle, her ray of sun, and her shoulder to lean on in her old age, a shoulder that she depends on more and more, she adds with a sigh. Nadia would never ever abandon her, she repeats many times, as if to convince herself, and would accompany her right up to the end of her days. But, but, with Mourad it was different. He was a man. He protected them. You always need the presence of a man in a house. Even if that man is still only a child. Not only because of all the jobs a man can take care of around the house. And with all that has been happening here, with all the strangers who wander around the camp at all hours of the day, with more and more thefts occurring, thefts that are becoming more and more daring, and with more and more attacks taking place, she is afraid. She, who has always lived by herself, without a husband or son, who never feared anything more than the jinn while living all alone at the far end of a garden in a little shed surrounded by plants and flowers, must now bitterly acknowledge that everything has changed today. It is as though all suppressed urges have found a way to come out, fully exacerbated by distress. Everyone has been seized by a form of unprecedented greed; unprecedented even for Dadda Aïcha, who has lived through wars, deprivation, and misery. No, it is more than that, she quickly corrects herself, it is rapacity, yes, that's a more precise word for it, an unlimited rapacity has seized hold of most of the individuals directly or indirectly affected by the catastrophe. Both those who have lived through it and those who live and profit by it without scruple, even if in order to do that, they have to despoil those who are most destitute. A rapacity that cancels out all generosity, sometimes even all feelings of humanity. With incoherent, contradictory behavior. Going from the most sincere compassion and active solidarity to the most maniacal egoism and inflexible harshness in the face of other people's hardships. As though each person, having had his fill of misfortune, having gone beyond the threshold of all tolerable suffering, had overdeveloped a survival instinct which, for some, was close to predatory. And, Dadda Aïcha adds in a weary tone, the earthquake has not only destroyed buildings and torn away thousands of people from the affection of their loved ones, but it has also shaken up all beliefs, perverted all behavior, and brought out all the most primal, most detestable, most odious aspects of human nature. And a return to the most ancient and strict religious traditions is for many but a chance to clear their own conscience. An absolution that doesn't cost much and is founded entirely on practices and practices alone—the most visible and most conspicuous possible. But God, for his part, knows what is hidden in the depth of people's hearts, she says, lifting her eyes up to the sky. He knows everything. And it is not by way of veils, prostrations, and invocations, noisy beyond all measure, that one can hope to mask the darkness and change the outcome of divine judgment.

In her remarks, there is no longer room for even the slightest ray of hope in man. I am profoundly shaken by the discouragement that Dadda Aïcha's words and gestures so clearly reveal. She seems to have let herself be won over by dejection, a form of mental and physical exhaustion that my words of reproach are powerless to change.

"You don't have the right to let yourself go like this. What about Nadia? She needs you. She is still young. You saved her. You saved us all. You took us under your wing, without asking any questions. You were there for us at the moment when we needed a helping hand—real affection and love offered without anything expected in return, since we arrived with nothing. You helped us accept ourselves and life. You gave us back our love of seasons, the desire to believe that all our tomorrows were possible. You even told us that all we needed to do was keep our eyes and our heart wide open for there to be light. These were your words. You taught us that all we needed to do was talk to trees and flowers for them to bloom. No, you don't have the right, this isn't like you at all . . ."

I'm insistent. I shake her. She remains passive, offers up no resistance, just smiles ever so slightly. As if all that I could say or do would never be able to reach her. I turn toward Dounya, who is sitting next to me on a mattress placed on the floor. She has been following the conversation without saying a word. She must feel very close to Dadda Aïcha right now. I can see it in the expression on her face, in the bitter folds that seem to have carved themselves in a little deeper at the corners of her mouth. Without thinking, I say:

"Say, what about if we took Dadda Aïcha and Nadia home with us? The house is big. And . . . there's the garden. It's totally abandoned. Dadda Aïcha could take care of it, she knows how. And I could help her. She would show me how. I'm sure it wouldn't be a problem. They would feel safe. Nadia could sleep with me, in the bedroom . . ."

At the very moment when I say her name, Nadia opens the door. She comes in. She screams with joy when she sees me and throws herself on me. She takes me in her arms passionately. I am a little surprised. I am not used to such demonstrations. It is true that we haven't seen each other for quite a while, but . . .

"I'm happy, so happy!"

She too has changed. She is radiant. The little room seems to be suddenly lit up by her presence alone. She is so full of the breath of life that I have a hard time recognizing her, a hard time finding in this girl, so obviously in full bloom and beaming with such youth, the wounded and reserved adolescent that I left here but several days before. I don't think the happiness that she is expressing so emotionally could be due to my presence alone. Everything—her gestures, her voice, the way she flashes her smile—everything about her communicates exaltation and an almost excessive enthusiasm in terrible contrast to the infinite sadness conveyed by Dadda Aïcha's attitude and words.

Nadia doesn't give me time to react. She hastily kisses Dounya on either cheek and, not bothering to pause long enough to answer her salutations, she grabs me by the hand, pulls me, makes me get up, and leads me outside.

ABOVE ALL, DON'T LOOK BACK

"There's something you have to, you absolutely have to know. I found Amine, yes, can you imagine, we found each other again. He had gone to stay with relatives in Algiers. And now he's here. He's back. He came looking for me. We saw each other again. We see each other every day. Dadda Aïcha has met him. I introduced him to her. She likes him, really likes him. You'll see . . . He . . . he is even more wonderful and even nicer than before."

I don't know who Amine is. All I can do is guess that he fulfills her life today. To the point of transforming her so radically that she is bursting with the desire to tell, to share her happiness with the whole world—she's so different from the stubborn, sullen, emotionally restrained girl I knew. Overwhelmed by her words, I grasp that she has known this boy for a long time. And even before. Before losing everything. I realize at the same time that this means she hasn't lost everything. And that it is this certainty which has metamorphosed her.

"You know, no you don't know, you wouldn't know, since I never told you, I was too ashamed . . . he was the one I was with on the day . . . the day of the earthquake. That is why I felt guilty . . . you understand now?"

There's no more trace in her voice of the emotion that tore her apart at the time when, profoundly shaken, she had evoked that day. She is freeing herself from her lie, facing my stupor with such casualness and utter lack of shame that it disconcerts me. She continues in the same tone.

"When you come to know what it is . . . but maybe you've already met someone, maybe you've already known a man and loved him, who knows. Maybe you're not even a virgin anymore. For my part, I gave myself to him. Entirely. Not like other girls, the ones who go out with a boy and flirt and who . . . who do everything with him, everything, except . . . you know what I mean? Because they want to keep their virginity to be able to find a husband. I think that's unworthy of love, of real love. But with us, with us it's not the same. Even if it is hard, very hard for us to see each other. There aren't many places around here to live out a love life. But we manage, one day here, one day there . . . And let me tell you, I love being in his arms more than anything else. I love it when he kisses me, when he touches me, when he lays his hands on me, when he caresses my hair, when he caresses my breasts. I love his smell, his skin, his eyes. I love to know he is overwhelmed and feverish at the idea of holding me against him, right up against him. Just think that I could have died, could have disappeared under tons of rocks without ever having experienced this!"

I listen to her in silence, stupefied by her unabashed confession. Nadia is seventeen years old. I would never have thought that a girl her age could speak so freely about her body, her most intimate feelings. There had been Sabrina of course, but . . .

"If you had experienced this, you would know it. Every fiber of your body would make you recall. No, this is something you wouldn't be able to forget. It's . . . it's as if you let yourself be overcome or utterly drawn under by a wave that is slow, warm, and full of such gentleness, violence, and intensity that it is exquisite, astonishing even—and you just let yourself go, not fighting it all, without being able or even wanting to struggle to escape, no, you don't want to escape, until you feel it rise up and spread inside you, this same gentleness, same violence."

Nadia has stopped. She is standing in the soft light of the autumn day, facing me. So distinct, so beautiful in the sun. It is only now that I notice the perfect harmony of her silhouette, the tranquil felicity that gives her gestures a new form of grace, her rounded hips snug in a fitted pair of jeans, her perky breasts, almost impudent beneath a skintight sweater, her hair with its warm brown highlights, falling freely over her shoulders.

Listening to her, looking at her, I have the impression of having hundreds, even thousands, of useless, sterile, hollow days behind me; I realize that for a very long time I have not been listening to my body. But have I ever been? I don't know. I'm not sure.

I'm disturbed by the unknown sensations and images Nadia's words arouse in me, Nadia's overwhelming beauty, her radiant fullness at this moment.

And then, I don't know why, my heart is suddenly gripped by uncontrollable anguish. As if I were afraid for her. As if, in the depths of my being, something told me that all happiness won by way of transgression must necessarily be in danger, must necessarily be unstable. As if I could not possibly believe she could so freely experience that sort of fulfillment, that sort of physical exultation, that sort of love. Before thinking "freely," I thought "with impunity." This doesn't really surprise me. I have known since the beginning—without even being able to situate the origin of this innate knowledge—the extent to which I am marked and corrupted by morals exclusively based on fault and sin, on punishment and expiation. All my efforts to make a clean slate of the repressive teachings, to erase the truths drilled into me, to eradicate and remove the precepts instilled in me, to forget and be reborn, in the end don't achieve a thing. Words, only words. I have been perverted. I think.

Nadia takes me by the arm and we turn back, in order to join Dadda Aïcha and Dounya, who have stayed together in the cottage. Before going inside, she holds me back at the threshold and plunges her gaze deep into mine:

"I don't care about how others see and judge me. I intend to see this all the way through, to live fully, to make eternity burst out of each instant, as if it were the last. It's the lesson I've learned from what we lived through here. The only lesson that's worth the effort of remembering. I am sure that my mother and Leïla, may God bless their souls, would understand me and would approve. Especially my mother. It couldn't be any other way. And do you know why? Simply because of love. Do you understand? When someone really loves their child, the only thing that should be important to them, no matter where they are, is knowing the child is happy!"

She sits down next to Dadda Aïcha, snuggling up beside her. She puts her arm around her shoulders, as if to protect her. And for the first time since I have seen her again, I see Dadda Aïcha's inimitable smile, full of tenderness and mischief.

ABOVE ALL, DON'T LOOK BACK

The roles are reversed.

It is Nadia now—made strong by the experience of love that is real and reciprocal—who reassures and protects Dadda Aïcha.

"It's as if you let yourself be overcome or utterly drawn under by a wave that is slow, warm, and full of such gentleness, violence, and intensity that it is exquisite, astonishing even—and you just let yourself go, not fighting it all, without being able or even wanting to struggle to escape, no, you don't want to escape, until you feel it rise up and spread inside you, this same gentleness, same violence."

Nadia's words resonate for me. They have reached a very obscure place in my memory and lodged there. I have not forgotten a single word of her declaration, which vibrated with a form of passion I have not yet encountered. I would certainly have remembered that . . .

It is not the first time that I have heard talk of this prodigious feeling of vertigo that she described so well, without false reserve, her face and body luminous, as though defying all the dark sides of humanity described by Dadda Aïcha. There were books of course, with real-life or imagined experiences, described in raw detail or else just suggested, usually by men—but it was a quite different reality. Women have alluded to it in front of me before, with meaningful smiles and long eloquent sighs. Allusion to that unnameable mystery which is invisible and elusive inside our very bodies, and which they will only evoke among themselves in covert phrases. What they call—whether it be out of a fear of words or else out of ignorance, I don't quite know—"that thing."

Almost in passing, Nadia made the following remark:
"I don't know if you are still a virgin." It wasn't really a question. Just a comment made in passing during the flow of conversation—no answer expected. I didn't know it was possible to talk about virginity in that way. With a lack of concern that lifts the weight of centuries of coercive moral decrees and alienating traditions from the word.

Something shivers in me and seems to float to the surface, with just the mere evocation of that, of . . . that thing. It has been an awful long time that I . . . that I haven't . . .

ABOVE ALL, DON'T LOOK BACK

An echo. A bit of music. At first, lighter than a prelude. A nervous sensation. Even excitement. At first, timid. A sort of entirely interior tremor that originates in the echo, in the words that I repeat in a low voice.

I am standing in my room. I am standing in front of the wardrobe's mirror. I am naked. I am looking at myself. I am discovering myself. I am discovering this body. Mine, without the slightest possible doubt. At the same time I am the observed and the observer. First with my eyes. Then with my hands. I discover my lips. A woman's lips. I follow their contour with the tips of my fingers. The soft and tender bulge of these closed lips. Still savage. Still sealed. And this curve. The place, both fragile and strong, where my neck connects to the rest of my body. My shoulders. I discover my arms. My breasts. My belly. My vagina. My thighs. My skin. With my fingers. I touch myself. I look at myself. I caress myself. A slow, gentle caress. That brushes over and then sometimes dwells in places, renders itself more precise. Ever so slightly. Brushes over skin. Brushes over consciousness. Carried along by the breath of my audacity, my desire is finally born and spreads out in long vibrating streaks. Shivers are born and are reflected in subtle waves over my belly and in the small of my back. A hollow pulsation is born inside me and joins with the beating of my heart, my heart that is thumping faster and faster.

I close my eyes. I don't want anymore.

Could it be that other hands have caressed me, have passed along my body? That they have brought to life in me a similar, similar trembling? That a man's hands have caressed me, slowly, as slowly, as tenderly, until . . . until . . . ? That other eyes have seen me as I see myself at this instant?

I don't see any trace.

I can't read any imprint or mark on this body of mine which has appeared strange and foreign to me ever since the day when the earth expelled its entrails. Yes, foreign, to the point of forgetting that it could be moved emotionally.

I don't know, I have never known what sensual pleasure is, except that which I am giving myself at this instant.

ABOVE ALL, DON'T LOOK BACK

It is now, only now that I understand the depth and destruction of forgetting.

And . . . standing in the middle of the room, there is this girl, Amina, looking at herself in the mirror, looking at me . . .

I don't need keys. Just turn the doorknob. The door opens. It wasn't locked. I think I knew it on the first day.

I walk into the room. It is as spacious as the living room on the ground floor. Dust and half-light. Beams of light flood through the closed shutters and stripe the tiling, the same tiling as in the rooms downstairs. In a corner, a wardrobe with a double door. A few chairs pushed up against the wall facing the door. Near the window, a piece of furniture, a dresser with three drawers that is a little larger than the one that is in *my* room. Placed on the dresser, a large bronze statue. Doubled in the large mirror that is hanging on the wall, just above. I have the very distinct impression that two absolutely identical women are facing each other. Two women down on their knees in a posture of begging, their arms held up to the sky.

I approach the dresser. The first drawer sticks a little when I pull to open it. Cardboard folders. Papers. Various documents: telephone, rent, gas, and electric bills. Everything classified and carefully filed away in envelopes. I read the name written on them. Yes, it's the name of Dounya's cousins. They have the same family name. Thus, they really did live here. I am holding the proof in my hands.

Then I open the second drawer. Placed one next to the other, there are photo albums, three large ones that are luxuriously bound. Golden threads on a green leather cover. In the albums, there are photos, a great number of them. I turn the pages, slowly. On each page, slid under a transparent plastic film, there are two or three photos. Most are black-and-white. The central character: Dounya. Beginning with a photo of Dounya as an adolescent, very angular and stiff, having visibly grown too fast, staring morosely at the camera. Then there is Dounya with her arm around an older woman who is undoubtedly her mother, for they have the same smile, the same gaze. Dounya in party attire, holding by the hand a little girl who resembles her, since they are dressed the same. Her sister Dalila, I presume. The aunt that supposedly took me in, raised me, and then disappeared at the very moment when we found each other again. Still more photos. Almost all are from the same period—a carefree age of friendship clearly on display. No sign of her early childhood. None of recent years either. One would say that there was only one period of her life that counted. That she wanted to remember only one. There are obviously blanks in her story.

I flip through each album one at a time and feel I am unlawfully entering a universe that is very different from what I know about her already. I have a hard time adjusting and making the two images of this person coincide, this person who is today so taciturn and secretive. I go over her life—a part of her life anyway—moment by moment. Here, standing at the edge of a beach, in a two-piece bathing suit, she is showing off a body that is very harmoniously shaped. And here again, sitting on a bench in what appears to be a university lecture hall, in the middle of a group of boys and girls, she appears to be discussing something energetically. Further along, she is standing at the edge of a wall wearing a very short skirt, and, with a mischievous look about her, she has tossed a big wool scarf back over part of her face. On certain pages, there are many white squares. Marks left behind by unglued photos. Photos have been taken out. In other photos, someone has cut out the faces.

Flipping through this series of captured and preserved moments, I come to realize that I know nothing about her. I know nothing about her life, except the things that she has willingly told me: her illness, her husband's death, then her mother's death, and more recently her sister's. She seems to have nothing more today than mourning and profound suffering. We have been living side by side for several days already, and I still haven't managed to pierce the opacity of her silence. Thus, I had never imagined that she had gone to university. Nothing in her conversation and behavior had suggested it to me, nor recalled the beautiful young inquisitive girl she must have been.

I would like to know more now. I search feverishly. I would like to find photos of Amina, the daughter, her daughter. Of the father who died prematurely and whom she never talks about.

ABOVE ALL, DON'T LOOK BACK

My heart is beating with such violence that I have the impression it will end up bursting right out of my chest.

I search. I have plenty of time. I know that Dounya won't come home early today. She told me she wouldn't.

For the first time since I have been living here, I heard the phone ring this morning. I heard her talking quietly, as though to make sure I wouldn't hear what she said. She was almost whispering. She spoke for a long time. The moment I stepped out of my room, she hung up. I was unable to read the expression on her face.

"Who was it?"

"Oh, nothing . . . no one . . . wrong number."

This is the first wrong number since my arrival.

I might have been able to believe her if she hadn't gone into her room a few minutes later and carefully closed the door behind her. I went and sat in the kitchen. I waited until she came out again. She appeared in the frame of the door and announced that she had to go downtown to take care of a problem. She added that I shouldn't worry if she was late. She was carrying a large bag. Something that resembled a binder or an attaché case, I couldn't see it very clearly. Normally, when she goes out, she doesn't bother to tell me why she is going out, where she is going, and at what time she will be home. It is all of these factors that have made me decide to go see the rooms upstairs, to go in search of answers to the questions I haven't dared to ask her.

I continue.

Third drawer. Three large red cardboard folders, without any title written on them. They are heavy. Full of papers. The edges of the folders are held together with adhesive tape, many strips of tape on each of the three sides.

I hesitate a little.

There they are, in front of me. What they have inside could certainly . . . At the same time, I tell myself that if she really didn't want for me to see them, she would have put them somewhere out of reach, under lock and key, in a safe place. I turn the folders over and over again in my hands. There is a certainty that beats inside me, whose source I can't explain, and I know that I am on the verge of a discovery, a revelation. I don't know, however, if I really want to lift the veil, to discover what she is hiding. Neither do I know if opening these folders will lead me to understand why she has erected impenetrable barriers all around herself, like someone who one day took a vow of solitude and silence. And yet, here I am. By her side. She came all the way to me. And I know she is capable of love, capable of giving, with sincerity and fervor that can't be doubted.

Nevertheless, there is something that holds me back. Not the fear of committing an indiscretion and then having to justify my curiosity, but a whole other fear, made at once of uneasiness and apprehension. It is as though I am standing at the very edge of an abyss, and as I feel irresistibly drawn toward the emptiness I am trying to keep my balance.

All I need to do is . . .

I slide the three folders into the drawer once again, very quickly, as if they were burning my hands.

I close the drawer. I leave the room without searching any further. Everything will resolve itself when she comes back. I prefer to wait a little while longer.

Can't you see, I have a better understanding of my fear now. This need I have, which can't be confessed, to put off the moment when I will have to open my eyes for real.

Dounya hasn't yet returned. She doesn't know I am waiting for her. That I waited for her all day. Night falls on the crests of the hills in the distance, then over the garden. Darkness thickens. Little by little, silence sets in. The birds that have been driven away by the night are seeking refuge elsewhere. I don't know where birds go when night falls. I never really thought about it. Maybe they don't leave at all. But instead they are always there, in the hollow of every branch, in every tree, perfectly still, waiting for the first signs of day. And that they just keep quiet, quite simply. They stop all their racket to let the world have its share of silence and the night its share of mystery. Dadda Aïcha used to say that in every living being on earth there is knowledge—an immemorial, instinctive understanding—of the necessary balance of the world. But many men, perverted by other forms of knowledge and the lust for power, have become altered from their natural state. They allow other instincts to act in them. And Dadda Aïcha was profoundly persuaded that it was certainly for this reason that the earth, feeling threatened, would from time to time fight back.

Dounya will perhaps not come back. I had never, before this instant, considered the possibility. To this barely formulated hypothesis, a profound conviction is immediately superimposed: she can't just disappear. From now on, our lives are closely interlinked.

Washed over with brisk gusts of cold air, night has gently slipped into every room, and I am shivering as I sit down next to the open window. I don't turn on the light. I contemplate the garden, just barely illuminated by a wan moon whose light outlines moving shadows all around. Dadda Aïcha hasn't come to bring it back to life, to talk to the trees, to give the plants their fair share of attention and tender care. They have subsisted nevertheless; left to the sun and the dryness, they are yellowing, shriveled, stunted, but still alive. Since I arrived, I have never once seen Dounya water them or even give them a little time.

ABOVE ALL, DON'T LOOK BACK

Nor have I myself. How easy it is to criticize in others what we so often fail to do ourselves!

I think I must have drifted off, my head resting against the cold windowsill.

I didn't hear the creaking of the gate.

I didn't hear the front door opening.

Dounya didn't turn on the light.

She is standing in front of me. I can only make out the form of her silhouette, a little more somber in the darkness.

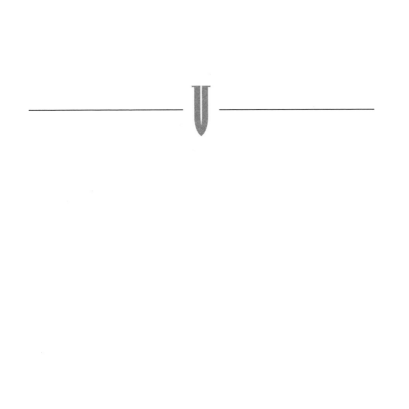

The moment has come to unravel the strings. To thus return to the advice that Dadda Aïcha gave me, do you remember that? Now I must go back over what Dounya, my mother, told me. So that I can tell you everything. Without forgetting a single word, a single pause, a single silence, a single exclamation. I could perhaps even give you indications with regard to her intonation, to the abrupt inflections in her voice, to the expressions that passed over her face.

And the tremendous racket in my head. The anger that words aroused in me. No, I must rectify. It was not anger. Is there a word for a storm that howls away inside you? A storm or a big wave made of whirling currents, of unchained fury, of swells, of disorder, of cries so piercing that men can't even hear them? Only dogs, perhaps, are able to. And these words . . . these words that stumble, bump, bang together, that repeatedly and violently ram into the inside of my skull . . .

Once again I am going to reenact the scene. One more time. But in a different manner, since I am one of the characters. A role for which I was not prepared.

"I have only one thing to ask of you," she says to me while pulling over an armchair to sit facing me. "I want, I would like very much for you to hear me out, all the way to the end, without interrupting me. Only speak if you have questions to ask me, if you want me to be more precise. But . . . hold on, hold on a minute, you're so cold, you're shivering . . ."

She holds my hands. Squeezing them between her own. "Wait, I'll bring you something, a sweater or a blanket. There is a good chance that the evening will be very long."

She leaves the room.

It is true that I'm freezing. I can't seem to subdue the shivering that is shaking my whole body. A long while later, she comes back. She hands me a big white wool shawl which I wrap around myself. Then she sits back down. Without turning on the light.

"I was just up on the second floor. When I was up there, I saw that you had found the photos. But you didn't open the red folders. I understood you were waiting for me, that you didn't want to go any further alone. I don't know if the moment has come, if you are ready, but . . . I can't wait any longer. I went ahead and completed all the necessary steps to be able to claim my documents, our documents. It took a very long time, and it was very difficult. But I have them now. No one can dispute it anymore . . . Before we look at the documents together, I have to tell you a story . . . I will start with the account of one day. One day only. You will understand right away which day is in question.

"On that day, I was set free from prison at twelve noon. They gave me back my belongings—my papers and my money. I signed the discharge from prison and I walked out. I didn't even have a bag. I had gathered everything I owned in a bundle made of a piece of red cloth that one of my cell mates had given me. I knotted the four corners as women used to do when going to the bath. Dalila knew. She was waiting for me. But she didn't tell you anything. That was agreed ahead of time. I was also aware of your schedule. That particular day, you were supposed to come home just after six o'clock. I had to be at her house, at your house, before you arrived home.

"As soon as the prison doors closed again behind me, I was overcome by a feeling of vertigo. A dizzy feeling that hasn't left me since. I had a hard time orienting myself in the city. Everything had changed. I walked through neighborhoods, entire quartiers that I didn't know. Everywhere I looked, I saw another construction zone: small and large buildings, villas, roads, sidewalks . . . construction going on everywhere and everything unfinished. Even the people themselves seemed different to me. Their way of behaving, their clothing, their way of looking at others, especially at women like me. But perhaps this was just an impression. And if you wonder why I'm going into all this detail, it is so you will understand why I wasn't able to follow you, to catch you.

"I walked around in the streets for a long time before finding a taxi. Taxis are rare now. I didn't know that. I gave the driver the address written on the paper that Dalila had given me, but it wasn't easy for him to find your apartment building amid all the new construction, all the new housing projects that don't have names or signs of any sort, their only designation being the number of housing units they include. He too had to drive around for a long time before dropping me off. I arrived at my sister's place at four thirty. You weren't there yet. And she had just got home from work. She cleaned various houses around the city in order to provide for the needs of the two of you. And when you were very little, you would often go with her to the houses where she worked. Before she had the means to rent her own apartment, you two even lived, for the longest time, in the house of one of her employers—a rich contractor with children the same age as you, twins I believe. As a matter of fact, it was thanks to his intervention that I was able to benefit from a reduction in my sentence. He is a member of Parliament now. You see, I know everything. When she came to see me, I asked her to tell me all that was going on with you. I wanted to know everything. Your grades at school, your friendships, the things that made you suffer, your dreams, everything that I couldn't share with you. She worked hard for you, for us, and outside of cleaning houses she wasn't able to get a job, despite her diplomas. For a large part because of me. Everybody knows about everything here. She would have had to leave the city. To have gone somewhere else with you, away, somewhere where she would have been able to live with the relative peace of mind of knowing herself to be anonymous once again. But I wouldn't have been able to stand having you far away from me. Dalila wasn't your mother. You knew that. We had decided to lead you to believe that your mother was dead. And that before dying she had entrusted you to her. And it was true in a way; I was dead, since I was forgotten, locked away in a place where I couldn't see you. And of course, many people will tell you that it is better to be dead than to be a criminal. What you didn't know was that your mother was never very far away from you. That I lived in a cell lined with your photos, with pages of your writing, with pictures you had colored in, with your drawings . . . that you were present everywhere.

"I realize now, too late, that this was perhaps the biggest error we made. Building your life on foundations of silence and then lies. But how to tell you that your mother was in jail? That she was condemned to twenty-five years in prison for a crime she had committed and admitted to? How to make you live with the infamy connected to the mere word prison? So it was that lying seemed a better option to us. To help you grow up carefree and innocent. So that you wouldn't have to pay for what I did. To encounter, your whole life long, the looks of curiosity and the hurtful remarks that you can guarantee would have been made by the men and women who knew.

"No, don't say anything. I asked you just to listen to me until I've finished. All the explanations you could possibly want, you will get. The documents are right there. We will read them together. The newspaper articles, the clippings that have to do with the case, everything is there. I kept them all. Dalila brought me everything that appeared in the newspapers about . . . about me, when she came to see me, and after that . . . after that I was given back my red bundle.

ABOVE ALL, DON'T LOOK BACK

"When you arrived . . ."

Her voice breaks. She buries her face in her hands. She is shaken with sobs. They are of such violence that she trembles all over.

I don't stand up. I don't go toward her. I can't move. Images come back to me. I don't want to grasp them though. Not yet. I allow them to slip past. They don't go very far. They just curl up calmly in a corner of the room waiting for me to recall them. I need to go all the way. For her to go all the way.

After a while, she lifts her head. Despite the dim light, despite the increasingly dense darkness closing in all around me, I can see the reddish shadows under her eyes and the puffiness of her face.

She continues in a firmer tone.

"When you arrived, it was after seven o'clock. You came in. You put your bag down on a little table in the entry hall. From where I was seated, I could follow every move you made in a mirror that was hanging on the wall, just in front of me. You slipped off the elastic that was holding back your hair. You shook your head, as if to loosen up your whole self. And the gracefulness of that movement leaped into my heart. It took you a while to notice that I was there. But when you saw me, you immediately smiled. You kissed me on either cheek without asking Dalila who I was. You didn't even notice the tears that I was unable to hold back upon seeing you. You were going to leave the room when Dalila called you back. When, pointing at me, she asked you if . . . if . . .

"You can't imagine, can't even imagine how many times I had dreamed of that moment while alone in my cell. I made that dream into the most beautiful film, the most original that had ever been made. I viewed the sequences over and over again, every night when the lights went out, amid the sound of yelling prisoners and insults being exchanged.

"You were standing right next to me. Looking at me with a glimmer of surprise in your eyes. You were probably a little perplexed because you had just become conscious of the emotion that was gripping Dalila and me. You must have read it on my face: the eagerness, the hunger, the need I had to hold you in my arms. Yes, you must have because you backed away a step. You shook your head. No, no, you didn't . . . you didn't know me, you had never seen me before.

"Dalila was the one who took everything too fast. And yet, we had talked things over for a long time before you got there. We had worked out a whole scenario that was meant to prepare you progressively, gently, for the revelation that would come. With questions and answers that would have led you make the deductions on your own.

"'This is Dounya. My sister. Your mother.'

"I still haven't understood why she revealed everything all at once, with such violence that she certainly must not have premeditated it. As if something in her had given way, so that she wanted to deliver herself of a burden that was suddenly too heavy to bear, and rid herself in two or three words of the weight of twenty years of silence.

"I could not bring myself to look at you at that moment. All I know is that you put your hand down on the table to hold yourself up. Out of fear of falling or to grab onto something that was solid, firm. And Dalila repeated:

"'This is her, this is your mother. She has come back.'

"I suppose that when you heard those words you must have immediately thought of an apparition, since you had grown up with the certainty that your mother was dead. Or of your aunt suffering from a sudden onslaught of insanity. Or more likely you thought of nothing at all and a vast emptiness took form in your head. I still couldn't lift up my eyes toward you. I too was utterly astonished.

"And then . . . then everything happened like in a film in slow motion. A totally different film from the one I had projected in my head so many times. I recall the sound of a very brief noise that escaped from you. Something like a hiccup, like a form of suffocation. I remember how you looked around. The panic that flooded your gaze. Only your eyes moved. You didn't move your head at all as you reexamined everything around you: the furniture, the paintings on the walls, the ornaments on the shelves one at a time, the curtains, the window, and farther away, the sky up above, as if to reassure yourself of their reality. From time to time, your eyes rested on me, but you seemed not to see me. I don't know how long this went on. An eternity . . . Dalila stood up. She went over to you, and it is at that very moment that you turned around all at once. In a single jerky movement, with your legs stiff as boards, you took three strides. You opened the door and ran out. I still have the noise of that race in my ears, the echo of your steps as you rushed headlong down the staircase. I hurried after you. I understood right away that something in you had just been tipped out of balance. I ran. You had already arrived on the ground floor when the earth started to rumble. Everything started shaking. I had just enough time to throw myself outside in order to avoid getting hit by the stones that had started to rain down all around. And then . . . I lost you, at the very moment when . . . but I already told you the rest the first time I saw you, when I finally managed to find you.

"So now you can understand why I didn't want to tell you the truth right away. Why I wanted to go easy on you, why I waited. Why I left the doors open. Why I didn't say a word. It was necessary to wait for the moment when you would be ready. I don't know yet if . . ."

I do believe that at that very moment I wanted to escape once again. I do believe that I heard the same subterranean rumbling, felt the same spells of dizziness, had the same impression of not being able to keep my balance on the earth and of being irresistibly drawn toward the immense night.

The press clippings are spread all over the floor. There are a lot of them. The case caused quite a stir in its day. Before going to bed, we didn't bother to pick them up. I gather them together, put them back in their red folder, and place them on the kitchen table.

My mother has been awake for a long time. She is in the rooms upstairs. I hear her walking around, moving furniture. I'm not sure what she's doing. Maybe cleaning up a bit.

I don't know what the best word would be for describing what she has become in the eyes of a society that has judged and condemned her for an act she committed more than twenty years ago, twenty-one years ago to be exact. Murderess, female offender. Is there a difference, I wonder, between the two terms. All I know is that they wouldn't be able to apply the term assassin, which is too exclusively masculine, to her.

The bill of indictment includes these words: guilty of voluntary homicide. With premeditation. Voluntary blows and injuries leading to death, as was the intention, according to the conclusions reached by the investigation. No mitigating circumstances, according to the members of the jury who had given their verdict. Twenty-five years in prison. For a coldhearted single-minded murderess who, according to the authors of articles reporting the case in detail, escaped the death penalty only because she had a little girl who was just two years old.

My father beat my mother. My mother killed my father. Said like this, it sounds like the last line in a chorus of a song, a bit like those chants that they taught us to repeat at school. The wolf bit the dog the dog bit the cat the cat scratched my father my father beat my mother my mother killed my father. And then we start all over again . . .

But it is not the same story. Only the last two propositions are true. At least that is the version taken up in the newspapers. My father beat my mother my mother killed my father.

"The case" is reported in impressively rich detail. Exactly as though the authors of the articles had been present at the scene of the drama and had witnessed the whole tragedy. In a living room, on the ground floor of a villa, a man grapples on the floor, bathed in his own blood. Next to him, a woman is seated in an armchair, pistol in hand, waiting for the day to dawn. A little girl is sleeping in her room a few meters away. All the facts are there, and the reasons barely mentioned: an argument that went sour, an exchange of blows, various forms of violence . . . The qualifiers, however, aren't lacking. Just one journalist mentions the marks left from blows and the numerous bruises found on the body of the little girl. All of them note Dounya's unshakable silence. She failed to utter a single phrase throughout all the hearings. Even her lawyer couldn't drag a single word out of her. She didn't respond to the attorney, to the examining magistrate, to the police officers in charge of the investigation, to the journalists, to the prison guards, to her cousins both male and female, nor to her fellow prisoners. And all the newspaper headlines that I have in view contain the same word: silence. In one, it is a question of "Strange Silence," in another, the "The Barriers of Silence," or else "Crime and Silence." And finally, the most remarkable of all: "Guilty Silence." Guilty, yes, she was. A woman who one night shoots her husband full of lead is guilty of a crime. There is no doubt about it. Especially when she goes and turns herself in to the police at the break of day, her little girl in her arms.

"I was waiting for her to wake up." This was the only phrase that she said when she arrived at the police station. But can it really be acceptable that even her very silence is subject to accusation?

As I skimmed over the various papers that she pulled out one at a time from the open folders, Dounya didn't try to explain further. I read almost everything. Then I put the papers down on my knees. I looked at her. It was at that very moment that I realized that her face had been transformed. The expression on her face. She appeared to be relaxed, relieved. It was like the wrinkles on her forehead and at the corner of her mouth had been miraculously wiped away. She appeared calm, mellower.

She began.

"To you and only to you, I am going to relate what happened on that night."

It was at that moment that I stood up. That I went over to her. I held out my hand toward her. She stood up in turn. She hesitated for a few seconds.

We looked at each other. Intensely. As though we had just now discovered one another.

Then she took me in her arms.

We were two. Mother and daughter.

We were reunited for the first time in over twenty years. Really reunited.

I held my hand over her mouth.

"No. No. I don't want to know. Hush now. Hush. Later. Later."

But tell me, tell me, doctor, I want to know for sure. What is there that is true in this story? You know about everything. You know all the characters. So it's up to you to tell me. It's up to you to unravel the strings. Who are the others? Where are the others? The father who is so powerful, so sure of himself . . . ? A creation, a projection? And the mother who is the exact opposite of my own? And the sisters who are twins, but why? A dual personality? And the brother so full of hatred and so easy to hate? Those men and women . . . It was all, all, according to you, but the product of mental confusion, of a disorder, of a scattering of consciousness? And this journey that has brought me toward you? It is true that in scientific language there exist terms that . . . Science knows everything, even if it can't predict everything. You know that all too well. Spatiotemporal disorientation you say? Following a psychological trauma that is so violent that it leads the subject to . . . , etc.

. . . a juxtaposition of places, times, and facts, where things don't quite line up, owing to the accumulation of two successive shocks, by the conjunction of two "events that are beyond my control"? Isn't that right? And I ought to believe you? So Wahida only existed for one summer? Isn't that what you would like me to admit . . . and Dadda Aïcha? Nadia, Mourad? All those people who are in my memory and in my story? What becomes of them? And Dalila? Why do I have no memory whatsoever of Dalila, who acted as my mother? Who can explain that to me? I don't know. I'm not sure. And this house that doesn't recognize me and that I don't recognize either. And now this immense wave that is rushing headlong, that is breaking, that . . .

AFTERWORD

Mildred Mortimer

The Algerian novel written in French is a product of the *fait colonial*, the French presence in a colonized nation. Following the conquest of 1830, French colonial settlers and administrators introduced the French language to Algeria; it reached a minority of indigenous Arabs and Berbers. Some were the children of families that saw an economic benefit in a French education; others were gifted students who, with little or no encouragement from illiterate families but with strong determination, intellectual ability, and good fortune, made their way through the French colonial educational system. Members of both groups figure among the first generation of Algerian writers: Mouloud Feraoun, Mouloud Mammeri, Mohammed Dib, Kateb Yacine. Several, including Feraoun and Mammeri, became educators themselves, teaching the next generation of Algeria's indigenous population.[1]

As a colonized nation, Algeria also had a cultural impact upon France. A new frontier to be visited, explored, and settled, it became a subject of literary inspiration. French writers such as Théophile Gautier, the Goncourt brothers, Eugène Fromentin, and Gustave Flaubert crossed the Mediterranean in search of exoticism, and wrote tales and travelogues inspired by their travels. The trend to depict Algeria through an Orientalist lens continued into the twentieth century, with metropolitan French writers such as André Gide turning to Algeria for escape from the quotidian. When, in the 1930s, Algerian writers of European descent, Albert Camus among them, formed the "Ecole d'Alger," they too tended to depict Algeria as an exotic landscape, rather than engage in a true encounter with the Other.

In contrast, the Francophone Algerian novel, from its early beginnings in the 1950s, rejected Orientalist stereotypes and clichés, choosing instead to reflect the authentic colonial experience, reaffirm the traditions of a precolonial cultural heritage, and express the quest for a new identity.[2] At first, a cautious description of daily life, as exemplified by Mouloud Feraoun's *Le fils du pauvre* (The poor man's son [1950]), the Algerian novel quickly became a cry of anguish and resentment. In this vein, Mohammed Dib's *La grande maison* (The big house [1952]) and Mouloud Mammeri's *Le sommeil du juste* (The sleep of the just [1955]) reflect the growing alienation of colonial subjects in the era marked by the end of World War II. Kateb Yacine's *Nedjma* (1955), however, refashioned the social realism that characterized the early texts by appropriating a form of poetic realism to explore myth, history, and the Algerian collective unconscious.

When Algerian women entered the anticolonial struggle, women's writing emerged as well. Assia Djebar first evoked the Algerian War in *Les enfants du nouveau monde* (Children of the new world [1965]), a text that depicts the growing political consciousness of Algerian women and their participation in the anticolonial struggle. Subsequent to Algerian independence in 1962, new political and social issues have emerged, and with them, a new generation of women writers. Djebar has called them the "nouvelles femmes d'Alger," new women of Algiers (*Oran*, 367), women who came upon the literary scene in the 1990s, using writing as a form of resistance against oppression.[3] Preoccupied with the unfavorable status of women in postcolonial Algeria, these new voices—including Maïssa Bey's—criticize the government's failure to promote a modern democracy that guarantees women's rights, and strongly oppose Islamic fundamentalists intent upon transforming Algeria into an Islamic state that would deny women their civil rights. Finally, by choosing to write in French, francophone Algerian writers, irrespective of gender, challenge their nation's active educational policy of arabization, which not only replaces French with Arabic, the national language, in Algerian schools but considers French a foreign language in Algeria.

AFTERWORD

From Samia Benameur to Maïssa Bey

With the growing interest among postcolonial writers in Africa's colonial history and its consequences, Algerian novelist Maïssa Bey has emerged an as important literary voice. Her texts—seven novels published within a span of twelve years (1996–2008)—center upon the violent and traumatic history of Algeria. In her work she delves into three critical historical periods: the French conquest of Algeria in 1830; the Algerian war for independence, 1954–62; the undeclared civil war between the Algerian government and Islamic fundamentalists of the 1990s.[4] Inspired to write during the turbulent 1990s, she situates her first text, *Au commencement était la mer* (In the beginning was the sea [1996]), in that period, addressing the issue of women's rights. A later work, *Entendez-vous dans les montagnes . . .* (Listen to one another in the mountains . . . [2002]), revisits the Algerian War via a train journey across France that serves as a symbolic place of memory for the daughter of an Algerian tortured and killed by the French and the French soldier (now a doctor) responsible for his death. Her latest novel, *Pierre sang papier ou cendre* (Stone blood paper or ashes [2008]), recalls the events of June 1830, when the French fleet invaded Algeria.

Born in 1950 in Ksar-el-Boukari, a village south of Algiers, Samia Benameur attended secondary school and university in Algiers, married, raised four children, and taught French in a high school in Sidi-bel-Abbès, the city in western Algeria where she still lives. When she began publishing her literary work in the 1990s, during the violent period of Algeria's undeclared civil war, Benameur was well aware of the dangers she faced. Despite the perils of challenging Islamic fundamentalists, she refused to wear the veil, continued to speak out against violence and repression, and chose to stay in Algeria. She did, however, assume a pen name to protect herself and her family. Selecting Maïssa, a first name her mother favored, and Bey, the surname of a maternal grandmother, the novelist turned to her maternal lineage to establish a public identity (*A contre-silence,* 32).

Bey was raised by her mother, who, after the assassination of her husband by the French security forces during the Algerian War, took care of her five children alone. The daughter of a bilingual legal counselor who later became a *cadi* (judge in the Muslim courts), she was fluent in French, having completed primary school and received her primary school certificate. Speaking of her mother's influence upon her, the novelist states:

> My mother was thirty, with five small children, when she was widowed. She never remarried. Despite all her suffering, she did not raise us in a culture of hatred for France and the French. But as a widow she was very frightened of the consequences of her behavior and afraid people would point the finger of blame at her daughters. The social pressure on women is tremendous. Women are under constant scrutiny from all sides. She was relieved to see us married. (Ruta)

To her mother's courage and determination in the face of hardship, her father added the dimension of political activism. During the early years of the Algerian War, Yacoub Benameur was a schoolteacher in Boghari, a village south of Algiers, and a militant in the FLN (National Liberation Front). In February 1957 he was arrested by French police, tortured, and executed. According to false newspaper reports in the local press, the "dangerous *fellagha* was slain by security forces while trying to escape" ("My Father," 27). Thus, Bey is the daughter of a *chahid,* a martyr to the Algerian War.

In a short memoir entitled "My Father, the Rebel," the novelist details her father's political activity and attests to an unwavering commitment to Algerian independence that labeled him a dangerous rebel and led to his death. She writes:

> When he joined the liberation movement in 1955, he was made a political officer in charge of providing logistical

support for the men in the *maquis*. He raised funds, delivered weapons and scheduled meetings of his cell right at his own father's farm located a few miles outside the village. For a long time he was able to carry out his assigned missions undisturbed, perhaps because he was well known but also because of the impression he made on those who barely knew him. Hard to imagine that this capable, honest and dedicated schoolteacher—as he was invariably described in the school superintendent's reports—this family man—five children already—would be capable of taking his wife and children to visit his parents' farm on a Sunday afternoon, in a car with a trunk load of weapons and ammunition. (27–28)

In another text, "Fragments," she recalls the night of her father's arrest:

I am pulled out of my sleep in the middle of the night. I hear footsteps. Voices. I open my eyes. There are men in the house. Three or four or maybe more. I don't know them. I have never seen them before. They are soldiers. They wear a green uniform with a big belt. They go from one room to the other. They don't speak to us. They don't look at us. All the lights are on. My mother is in her nightgown. She has my little brother in her arms. He's asleep. My big brother is standing next to her. The soldiers open all the doors. All the drawers. Even those in my father's study. They throw everything they find on the floor. I don't see my father. (73; translation mine)

Readers may be surprised by the terse style the author adopts to depict an event this emotionally charged. This minimalist style, however, suggests that words fail to convey the trauma experienced by the family at this moment. By presenting the event from a child's perspective, Bey recovers the tragic moment, yet reveals the child's inability to fully comprehend its significance.

In this same text, she returns in memory to the empty classroom following her father's arrest. Here, she evokes his martyrdom as a collective as well as a personal experience. Her father was the community's schoolteacher; his loss extends beyond the family. She writes: "I am in my father's classroom. The room is empty. There are no students, no teacher. My father's gray smock hangs from the coatrack near the door. I smell the scent. I close the door. I leave the room. I leave the school. I leave behind the child I once was" (74; translation mine).

Bey acknowledges that places are always complex constructions of personal and interpersonal experiences. If, as Victor Walter notes, meaningful places are containers of experience, capturing experience and storing it symbolically, such places also provide road maps for the future. Thus, by returning to the schoolroom, where she draws the reader's attention to an artifact, the grey smock the schoolteacher—her father—will never again pick up from the coatrack, the novelist suggests that her father's martyrdom was a crucial element in her own development as an educator, writer, and political activist.

Significantly, her father's relationship to the French language determined, in large measure, her own. He moved beyond the world of his illiterate peasant family and, in so doing, came to value the French language even as he encountered the contradiction between the ideals of the French Revolution, with its concepts of liberty, equality, fraternity, and the inferior political, economic, and social status attributed to colonial subjects. If, as she notes, "My father's death brought the war into my life" ("My Father," 27), his life, specifically his role as an educator within the French colonial system, encouraged her vocation as a francophone writer. Thus, the novelist comes to literature with a personal connection to the collective trauma that accompanied the liberation struggle; violence took her father's life but not his vision for his country. It left his family with the legacy of trauma and yet a belief in a better future for Algeria.

When violence occurred again in Algeria in the 1990s, this time within the country, claiming the lives of over 120,000 people, including intellectuals—writers, journalists, scientists, doctors—it forced many secular French-educated professionals into exile. Bey, however, remained in the country, fought for her intellectual ideals, and embarked upon her literary career. Nevertheless, the death of her friend and colleague Salah Chouaki, shot in his car on his way to work in September 1994, was very difficult for her and marked a turning point: "After his death, I began to write my first novel" (Ruta, 3).

This first novel, *Au commencement était la mer,* gives readers a privileged view on the issues that concern Algerian women, particularly the young today. Her protagonist, Nadia, is an Algerian student who, after a brief love affair that results in pregnancy, has a clandestine abortion. Her confession to her brother, an Islamic fundamentalist, leads to her death at his hands. With this work, Bey established herself as a politically committed writer whose focus is upon the myriad problems of postcolonial Algeria—poverty, corruption, misogyny, Islamic fundamentalism—particularly the status of women.

The political engagement she expresses in her writings extends to political action; it led her to establish Paroles et Ecriture, an association founded in 2001 to promote women's writing. Adapting the format of *ateliers d'écriture* (reading and writing workshops), she encourages Algerian women to tell their tales, write their stories, and use writing as a tool for empowerment and social justice. Paroles et Ecriture recently won an important victory, the establishment of a new library. In 1990, when Islamic fundamentalists won the municipal elections in Sidi-bel-Abbès, they shut down the public library. More than a decade later, the group obtained a grant from the European Union to build a new one.[5]

Earthquakes in Algeria: Reality and Metaphor

Earthquakes have been comparatively frequent occurrences in the intensely earthquake-prone area of the country, between the northern slopes of the Atlas Mountains and the southern coastline of the Mediterranean Sea, where the majority of the country's population of 30 million people is concentrated. In 1716 the city of Blida was destroyed and more than 20,000 inhabitants lost their lives. More than a hundred damaging earthquakes have been recorded since then, all in the area north of the Atlas Mountains, and most of those in the region west of the capital city of Algiers. In modern times, Orléansville (the former name of El Asnam, now renamed Chleff) suffered a major earthquake in 1954, was rebuilt, and destroyed by another major earthquake in 1980.[6]

Algeria's most recent earthquakes occurred in May 2003, on three days, the 21st, 27th, and 29th. They damaged Algiers as well as towns east of the capital. Many buildings were destroyed, particularly in the poor sections of Algiers: Bab-el-Oued, Belcourt, and the Casbah. The first of the three quakes measured 6.7 on the Richter scale, the next two 5.8. According to published reports, they resulted in the deaths of 2,251 people, with another 1,200 missing and 200,000 left homeless.[7] In Algiers, a city in which a housing crisis persists and where water shortages are common, people questioned why some buildings withstood the shock and others fell apart. Many pointed fingers at dishonest contractors, whom they accused of pocketing profits by using inexpensive building materials, resulting in extensive damage to buildings that should have withstood the tremors. At the same time, Islamic elements began accusing "infidels" of bringing the wrath of God upon them through irreverent behavior in their daily lives.

Above All, Don't Look Back takes place in the aftermath of the three earthquakes of 2003. Depicting the death, devastation, and disorientation that resulted from the quakes and aftershocks, Bey anchors her text in Algerian reality. However, by dedicating her novel not just to Algeria's victims but to Asia's victims of the tsunami of 2004 as well, she suggests that her readers grieve for *all* victims of natural disasters. Although inspired by the events of 2003, she insists upon the fictional nature of the work—"the entirely fictitious characters inhabiting these places could bear a resemblance to existing or previously existing people" (1)—thereby encouraging symbolic interpretations of the text. On the one hand, earthquakes may represent all forms of violence that have been part of the Algerian history since the colonial conquest of 1830. On the other hand, they may be viewed as catalysts for personal transformation, traumatic events that nevertheless encourage survivors to envisage a new order, perhaps a new view of themselves and their world.

The second interpretation, I believe, best defines the novel. Structured as a three-part narrative, it begins with Amina, the protagonist/narrator, walking dazed through the rubble of her city following the first quake. The trauma she experiences that day leads the young woman to break with her former life. Refusing a marriage arranged by her family, she flees from home. Her outward journey is interrupted by a second earthquake; it leaves her unconscious and suffering from amnesia. Rescuers place her in a refugee camp, where, with the help of fellow survivors, she begins to construct a new life. Yet her world is jolted again when a woman who claims to be her mother enters the camp. As the novel ends, Amina, still unable to recollect her past, searches for clues that will help determine whether the woman who has taken her "home" is indeed her mother, and whether the woman's account of their former life, together and apart, is truthful.

Depicting a world turned upside down as the result of a natural disaster, and a protagonist whose amnesia results from the trauma, Bey introduces themes in her novel that have become increasingly important in contemporary literature: trauma and memory—its loss, misrepresentation, and recovery. Addressing trauma, the novelist situates her text within a body of contemporary works that includes literature of the Holocaust, the Rwandan genocide, the anticolonial wars of Vietnam and Algeria. In her study of trauma, Maria Tumarkin applies the term "traumascape" to places scarred by violence, war, and terror, and explains that people who experience a traumatic event are often so overwhelmed that "the ways in which they usually experience the world and make sense of their own place in it are effectively shattered" (11). Working with Freudian concepts, Cathy Caruth defines trauma as a wound: "It is always the story of a wound that cries out, that addresses us in the attempt to tell us of a reality or truth that is not otherwise available. This truth, in its delayed appearance and its belated address, cannot be linked only to what is known, but also to what remains unknown in our very actions and our language" (*Unclaimed Experience*, 4).

Focusing on its delayed appearance (which Freud calls latency) and its recurrence, Caruth identifies trauma as "unclaimed experience" that "possesses" the traumatized. In other words, because of its unassimilated nature, it continues to haunt the survivor. Further, by noting the difficulty involved in establishing the truth surrounding a traumatic event, Caruth reveals the paradox "that in trauma the greatest confrontation with reality may also occur in an absolute numbing to it, that immediacy, paradoxically enough, may take the form of belatedness" (ibid., 6). The ability to recover the past is paradoxically linked to the inability to have access to it. In Bey's text, we find a traumatized protagonist struggling with her inability to reach the truth, and questioning her reliability as a narrator. Throughout her narrative, Amina wonders—as do her readers—where the truth of her experience lies.

Engaging the theme of memory, Bey joins historians and writers for whom it is central to understanding postcolonial Algerian society. Benjamin Stora, a leading historian of the Algerian War, contends that the state of amnesia surrounding the events of the war has harmed France and Algeria. In *La gangrène et l'oubli*, he labels repressed memories of the Algerian War a form of gangrene sapping the foundations of French society. He warns that neither communities nor individuals can "exist and define their identity in a state of amnesia" (319; translation mine). In this same vein, Algerian writers have begun uncovering hidden histories of French colonial conquest and the Algerian War. When Assia Djebar delved into French colonial history pertaining to the conquest of Algeria, she uncovered a "forgotten" incident of *enfumade,* the French military tactic of setting caves on fire to asphyxiate Algerian tribes taking refuge in them. The novelist came to view herself as a spelunker, an underground explorer engaged in "a very special kind of speleology" (*Fantasia,* 77). Her exploration of Algerian history led her to reexamine events of the Algerian War, thereby "unearthing" the story of Zoulikha, a martyr to the independence struggle who lived and died in Djebar's native region of Cherchell.[8] Bey, in turn, extends the speleological quest to the 1990s. Charting Amina's struggle to recover her past, she alerts readers to the importance of historical accuracy with respect to Algeria's undeclared civil war. Interweaving a fictional narrative with national history, she takes a stand against silence and denial, the "voluntary amnesia" that contributes to injustice and denies human rights.

Leaving Home

Amina's words "I walk through the streets of the city" (7) introduce her encounter with the death and destruction that have come to her city in the wake of the earthquake. As witness to the disaster, she comments upon the odor that permeates the city, the efforts of rescuers to recover trapped victims, the signs of destruction: twisted electric poles, disoriented birds, swarming flies. The experience is overwhelming for her. She says: "An entire lifetime wouldn't be enough time to tell what I've seen. What I am seeing. Speak up or remain silent forever" (8).[9] Describing a shattered world, she acknowledges that the disaster has transformed her emotionally: "I'll no longer be the girl I was" (8). What begins as an encounter with a natural catastrophic event will become a journey to empowerment.

Upon reaching home, Amina discovers that her house has suffered little material damage: some cracks in the walls, a few broken glasses in the sideboard, and a "fallen picture of father, framed and enlarged, showing him next to the president of the

Republic, who had come to inaugurate the construction zone for a new subsidized housing project" (20). She concludes that her family has escaped unscathed.

Has she misjudged the impact of the tremor? The house has been spared, yet traces of disintegration are apparent. Her father, a rich entrepreneur in the construction business with strong ties to the government, may soon be accused of pocketing money for housing projects that, had they been built with proper materials, would have withstood the tremors. Furthermore, when his daughter disappears from home on the eve of her marriage, he risks social humiliation and ridicule. Hence, in both literal and symbolic terms, the father's fallen picture can be interpreted as the beginning of the end of the patriarchal order. Later, Amina sketches a portrait of her father that clearly reveals his weaknesses: "Main character. Due to his role as parent and uncontested head of the family, but also due to his portliness. He takes up the entire stage. Close-up of his face distorted with anger. His bloodshot eyes. The quivering of his upper lip. His nervous stuttering, revealing unusual dismay" (39). On the one hand, she acknowledges her father's dominant place in the family ("He takes up the entire stage"). On the other hand, she undercuts his power. Foregrounding the anger that distorts his features—his lips quiver and he stutters nervously—she shows how his anger diminishes his authority. It is a weakened patriarch who invents the lie that his daughter has been abducted from their home and never asks himself, nor any of the family members who join him in spreading the lie, why the young girl has run away from home.

Why does she run away? The answer lies in the conflict between her quest for autonomy and her parents' belief in patriarchal authority, including the right and obligation to arrange her marriage. It is interesting to note in this regard that her mother is guardian of the meticulously kept house; she, like her husband, is wedded to the world of appearances. By leaving home, Amina rejects the house of patriarchy, turning her back on a family that is oppressive. Confirming this interpretation of Amina's relationship to her home, Carole Boyce Davies finds that in women's writing of Africa and the African diaspora, home is often a place of alienation, and the family, a site of oppression (21). The critic emphasizes the importance of leaving home: "Home can only have meaning once one experiences a level of displacement from it" (113).

Judith Fryer's reflections upon women's relationship to domestic space are pertinent here as well. She writes: "The structures that contain—or fail to contain—women are the houses in which they live, the material things of their lives, and the illustrations and stories that instruct them in ways of perceiving themselves and relating to others" (64–65). The three elements—house, material objects, stories—contribute to a woman's sense of "her place" in the world. In Bey's text, the earthquake that has shaken the foundations of several Algerian cities has weakened Amina's relationship to the patriarchal structure that has "contained" her. She is now able to leave it behind. Significantly, before crossing the threshold, she looks at herself "one last time" in the mirror that hangs over the dresser near the doorway. As she opens the door, she takes leave of her former self.

Crossing the threshold, Amina takes the first step toward creating a new self and embarks upon her journey of self-discovery. Closing the door gently behind her, she affirms her independence as she defies the patriarchal code that keeps women under male control. Bringing house imagery—a closed door—to bear upon the process of psychological growth, Bey recalls the work of Gaston Bachelard, whose study *The Poetics of Space* depicts house imagery as contributing to the individual's increased self-awareness. Using a door to reflect upon the relationship between freedom and security, Bachelard asks a rhetorical question: "But is he who opens the door and he who closes it the same being? The gestures that make us conscious of security or freedom are rooted in a profound depth of being" (224). Probing the symbolic meaning of the gestures of opening and closing a door, he alerts us to the dynamic relationship that exists between open/closed, outside/inside spaces.

Making a Home in the Cracks

As the first part of the novel introduces the harsh reality of a ravaged city, the second takes us to the refugee camps. Here, traumatized individuals who have lost family, friends, and shelter struggle to survive and to find meaning in lives that have been badly shaken. Emphasizing the importance of women in responding to the crisis, Bey introduces Dadda Aïcha. Poor, aged, and illiterate, she emerges as a heroic figure in the camp, creating a family by assembling a group of young refugees around her. They include Mourad, a fiercely independent adolescent who dreams of leaving Algeria for a better life in Europe; Nadia, a high school student who hopes to take her university entrance exams; and Amina, who has lost the link to her past. The "three lost dogs with no collars" (77), as Amina calls them, find common ground as survivors of a traumatic event and join Dadda Aïcha in the creation of a new family.

Examining the effects of trauma upon communities, Kai Erikson finds a spiritual kinship among people who have shared a catastrophic event. He notes that "trauma shared can serve as a source of communality in the same way that common languages and common backgrounds can" (186). In Amina's life, the sense of community begins in the camp. Having experienced isolation and loneliness in the home she fled, she comes to value the tent village as her true home. Despite the difficult conditions it presents in terms of food and lodging, the refugee camp offers "a home in the cracks."[10] It defines a transitional space that is open, fluid, and promises new possibilities for the future because of the spiritual kinship that the catastrophic event has forged.

In her study of third world women's writing, Davies notes the importance of female elders to the process of female empowerment, specifically their unique role in communicating the knowledge of healing arts, nurturing, memory, and survival skills to younger women. Her analysis is pertinent to Bey's novel, in which Dadda Aïcha saves Amina's life and then encourages her journey to self-understanding and empowerment. As Amina explains, Dadda Aïcha found her "lying lifeless on the road—curled up, ice-cold, stiff—so stiff that at first she thought there was nothing that could be done for me, that I was gone" (51). When she realizes that Amina is alive, she forces her to drink some water, "drop by drop, like you get a baby to drink" (52).

As she brings the young girl back to life, the old woman establishes emotional bonds with her and becomes, in effect, the nurturing maternal figure Amina seems never to have known. In this role, she names her Wahida, a name with three meanings in Arabic: first, unique, alone. If Amina's new name reflects the state of solitude she experiences as an amnesiac, her plight may also be interpreted within a broader context as the struggle of postcolonial Algeria to find its identity in a complex world of competing and conflicting ideologies.

In the refugee camp, not only does Dadda Aïcha fill the role of female elder, she is also the voice of collective memory. Telling stories of bygone days, she recalls the colonial past the young have not shared with her. Conveying a sense of nuanced nostalgia, she explains that under French rule there were injustices and discrimination, but also an art of living and a love of nature, which in her view has disappeared: "Now wrought-iron bars, metal cisterns, and satellite dishes are all that can be seen" (67). Assuming a critical voice, she cautions Algeria to reestablish its links to the land, thereby articulating the writer's concerns. The novelist speaks through her protagonist to warn against the loss of community, and to urge respect within the community for one another's beliefs.

Putting the Pieces Back Together

In a fascinating book about World War I, *The Living Unknown Soldier: A True Story of Grief and the Great War,* Jean-Yves Le Naour re-creates the story of an amnesiac soldier. Anthelme Mangin, as he was later called, was found wandering along the platform of a French railway station in 1918 after a convoy of returning prisoners had passed through; the soldier never recovered his memory. Mangin came to stand for the suffering of the families of the missing. When French authorities placed advertisements calling for the soldier's family to come forward, thousands of families attempted to claim him.[11] Bey's text mirrors this haunting story by introducing a dramatic element: the arrival in the camp of a woman who claims to be another amnesiac's mother.

It is not surprising that Amina cannot recognize the woman who claims to be her mother. Throughout the period spent in the refugee camp, she continues to show signs of mental confusion, admitting: "The words I decipher resist me fiercely. Characters elude me. Plots get muddled," and she adds:

> In a similar way, when I wake up in the morning, it takes me a long time to put the pieces of my story back together. To figure out exactly where it is that I am, and to integrate myself back into reality. It is as though a jinni— a cunning little spirit, one of those Dadda Aïcha thinks she sees lurking around us—were taking advantage of the time when I sleep to torment me, to scatter my dreams in disparate shards, and to hold me back at the break of day so that I can't open up my eyes fully and move toward the light. (61)

Accompanying the woman home, Amina embarks upon the next part of her journey. Leaving the camp, she in effect gives up the dream of creating her own destiny. However, by accepting Dounya's offer of a home, she opens the possibility of acquiring the personal history that has so far eluded her. Yet, when she arrives at the new home, Amina senses that her presumed mother is keeping a secret from her. As she searches through her mother's drawers in an attempt to retrieve clues to her elusive past, Amina is torn between the desire to find the key that will unlock the door to the past, and the fear that this knowledge will bring more suffering. Rather than open her mother's personal archives, she waits for Dounya to speak.

Dounya surprises Amina and the reader by disclosing a traumatic story of child abuse. She explains that she murdered her husband, Amina's abusive father, to protect her child, and subsequently served a long prison sentence for the murder. Amina, in her mother's absence, was raised by her aunt, Dalila, who kept the secret, telling her niece she was an orphan. The day Dounya was released from prison and reunited with her daughter, the earthquake struck, killing Dalila and robbing Amina of her memory.

This narrative, if true, explains an earlier passage in the text that we may now consider a traumatic flashback. As Dounya approaches Amina in the refugee camp, Amina describes a vision that is possibly a repressed memory:

> Unexpected and violent as the stab of a knife, an image flashes before my eyes of a little girl so terrified that although she wants to scream, no sound escapes from her mouth; a little girl in tears, overwhelmed by fear and pain, driven back against a wall by a man whose face, whose fists are threatening her. Where? When? I don't know. I'm not sure. Only the suffering and fear remain intact. And a terrible feeling of helplessness that, at this instant, sweeps away and annihilates all desire, all capacity to resist. (103)

If Dounya's account of abuse and murder is accurate, her daughter's amnesia is rooted in a double trauma: the return of the mother she was unprepared to meet which jolted repressed memories; the earthquake that left her unconscious and barely alive.

Although Dounya's narration is a plausible explanation of events, it nevertheless poses questions of authenticity and identity. Who is Amina? Is she the daughter of the rich contractor? Was she running from an arranged marriage when the earthquake struck? Is she the daughter of a woman who committed murder to protect her from her violent father? Was she running from the mother she was not prepared to meet? If the first part of the novel is a fiction, what of the second? Are Dadda Aïcha, Nadia, and Mourad "real" or "fictional"? And finally, why does Amina have no memory of Dalila, the aunt who raised her, nor of the house that had been their home?

As Bey leaves her readers with unanswered questions, Bachelard's reflections on the concept of home are relevant. Adults, he explains, find comfort in the present by reliving memories rooted in childhood space. This childhood home may no longer exist in reality, but it remains in one's memory. Amina, however, like the living unknown soldier Anthelme Mangin, has no such memories. When she fled from impending disaster, she saved her life. Yet, as Caruth's study of "unclaimed experience" reminds us, trauma often "possesses" the survivor. Bey, whose own life experiences include the trauma of her father's arrest, torture, and death when she was a child, leaves us to ponder the consequences of personal and collective trauma. Her novel reframes Caruth's theoretical work and probes the same question: How does an individual, a community, or a nation negotiate between the story of the unbearable nature of an event and the story of the unbearable nature of surviving it? This is a key question for Bey, her readers, and her nation to continue to explore.

NOTES

1. It is important to note that the fathers of several prominent Algerian women writers were teachers as well: Tahar Imalayen (Assia Djebar), Mohammed Sebbar (Leïla Sebbar), Yacoub Benameur (Maïssa Bey). Significantly, all three women novelists have evoked their father's influence upon their development as writers. See Djebar, *Fantasia, an Algerian Cavalcade,* and Sebbar, *Je ne parle pas la langue de mon père.* For Bey, see "Fragments," and "Mon père, ce rebelle."

2. Pre-Independence Francophone writing can be traced back to 1920 and the publication of Mohamed Ben Chérif's autobiographical novel *Ahmed Ben Mostapha, goumier.* This text, the autobiographical

work of an Algerian who joins the French army in 1899, is now available in a 1997 reprint with an introduction by Ahmed Lanasri.

3. For studies of contemporary Algerian women's writing, see Ireland.

4. Amnesty International issued a report in 1996 that noted 50,000 deaths attributed to the civil war. A report in the *New York Times*, August 20, 2008, A8, placed the death toll at 150,000. Although the period of violence appeared to have ended in the first years of the new millennium, terrorist attacks have begun again. A new terrorist group, Al Qaeda in the Islamic Maghreb, appeared in 2006. It has taken responsibility for the deadly attack on the United Nations headquarters in Algiers in December 2007, as well as bomb attacks in spring and summer 2008.

5. The library in Sidi-bel-Abbès is building collections in several languages, including English and French. Supporters may send books to Bibliothèque Paroles et Ecriture, 17, rue Aissat Idir, 22000 Sidi-bel-Abbès, Algeria. The e-mail address is paroleécriture@yahoo.fr.

6. For a study of the Orléansville earthquake as a catalyst for social transformation and political reform in French colonial Algeria, see Fletcher.

7. For further information about these earthquakes, see James Lewis, "The Algerian Earthquakes of May 2003: Some Precedents for Reconstruction," http://www.radoxonline.org/algeria2.htm.

8. Zoulikha's burial site remained unknown until 1984, hence the title of Djebar's novel, *La femme sans sépulture*, "the woman without a tomb." Before publishing this novel, Djebar presented the story of Zoulikha in her film *La nouba des femmes du Mont Chenoua* (1977). In this same vein, Leïla Sebbar's speleological endeavor also involves repressed memory of an incident that occurred during the Algerian War. Her text, *The Seine Was Red*, evokes the massacre of Algerians in Paris on October 17, 1961.

9. With Amina's words "Speak up or remain silent forever," Bey refers to the Algerian writer Tahar Djaout, the victim of Islamic fundamentalist terrorism. Shortly before he was fatally wounded in May 1993, Djaout wrote:

Silence is death,
And if you speak out, you die,
And if you remain silent, you die.
So, speak and die. (Dakia, 38)

In Dakia's text, Djaout's verse appears on a banner carried through the streets of Algiers.

AFTERWORD

10. I am borrowing this expression from Marie-Denise Shelton, who uses it in her study of Haitian women's ability to create and preserve the sense of home in diasporic space (77).

11. Jean Anouilh used Anthelme Mangin to create the hero of his play *Le voyageur sans bagage,* staged in 1937, when Mangin was surrounded by experts trying to decide among the various families who claimed him as their relative.

BIBLIOGRAPHY

Amnesty International. *Algérie*. Paris: Amnesty International, 1996.

Anouilh, Jean. *Traveller without Luggage*. Trans. of *Le voyageur sans bagage* by John Whiting. London: Methuen, 1959.

Bachelard, Gaston. *The Poetics of Space*. Trans. Maria Jolas, with a foreword by John R. Stilgoe. Boston: Beacon Press, 1994. First published as *La poétique de l'espace*. Paris: PUF, 1957; repr. 1984.

Ben Chérif, Mohammed (Caïd). *Ahmed Ben Mostapha, goumier*. 2nd ed. Paris: Publisud, 1997.

Bey, Maïssa. *A contre-silence*. Grigny: Editions Paroles d'Aube, 1998.

———. *Au commencement était la mer*. Paris: MARSA, 1996.

———. *Bleu blanc vert*. La Tour d'Aigues: Editions de l'Aube, 2006.

———. *Cette fille-là*. La Tour d'Aigues: Editions de l'Aube, 2001.

———. *Entendez-vous dans les montagnes . . .* La Tour d'Aigues: Editions de l'Aube/Algiers: Editions Barzakh, 2002.

———. "Fragments." In *Mon père*, ed. Leïla Sebbar. Montpellier: Editions Chèvre feuille étoilée, 2007. 65–74.

———. "My Father, the Rebel." Trans. by Suzanne Ruta. *World Literature Today*, November 2007, 27–30. First published as "Mon père, ce rebelle," in *A contre-silence*, 80–90.

———. *Pierre sang papier ou cendre*. La Tour d'Aigues: Editions de l'Aube, 2008.

———. *Sous le jasmin la nuit*. La Tour d'Aigues: Editions de l'Aube, 2004.

———. *Surtout ne te retourne pas*. La Tour d'Aigues: Editions de l'Aube, 2005.

Caruth, Cathy. "Introduction: Trauma and Experience," and "Introduction: Recapturing the Past." In *Trauma: Explorations in Memory*, ed. Cathy Caruth. Baltimore: Johns Hopkins University Press, 1995. 3–12; 151–57.

———. *Unclaimed Experience: Trauma, Narrative, and History*. Baltimore: Johns Hopkins University Press, 1996.

Dakia. *Dakia, fille d'Alger*. Paris: Castor Poche Flammarion, 1996.

Davies, Carole Boyce. *Black Women, Writing, and Identity: Migrations of the Subject*. London: Routledge, 1994.

BIBLIOGRAPHY

Djebar, Assia. *Fantasia, An Algerian Cavalcade.* Trans. Dorothy S. Blair. London: Quartet Books, 1985. First published as *L'amour, la fantasia.* Paris: Jean Lattès, 1985; Paris: Albin Michel, 1995.

———. *La femme sans sépulture.* Paris: Albin Michel, 2002.

———. *Oran, langue morte.* Arles: Actes Sud, 1997.

Erikson, Kai. "Notes on Trauma and Community." In *Trauma: Explorations in Memory,* ed. Cathy Caruth. Baltimore: Johns Hopkins University Press, 1995. 183–99.

Fletcher, Yaël Simpson. "The Politics of Solidarity: Radical French and Algerian Journalists and the 1954 Orléansville Earthquake." In *Algeria & France, 1800–2000: Identity, Memory, Nostalgia,* ed. Patricia M. E. Lorcin. Syracuse: Syracuse University Press, 2006. 84–100.

Fryer, Judith. *Felicitous Space: The Imaginative Structures of Edith Wharton and Willa Cather.* Chapel Hill: University of North Carolina Press, 1986.

Ireland, Susan. "The Algerian War Revisited." In *Memory, Empire, and Postcolonialism: Legacies of French Colonialism,* ed. Alec G. Hargreaves. Lanham, MD: Lexington Books, 2005. 203–15.

———. "Voices of Resistance in Contemporary Algerian Women's Writing." In *Maghrebian Mosaic: A Literature in Transition,* ed. Mildred Mortimer. Boulder, CO: Lynne Rienner, 2001. 171–93.

Le Naour, Jean-Yves. *The Living Unknown Soldier: A True Story of Grief and the Great War.* Trans. Penny Allen. London: William Heinemann, 2005. First published as *Le soldat inconnu vivant.* Paris: Hachette, 2002.

Ruta, Suzanne. *The Rebel's Daughter: Algerian Novelist Maïssa Bey.* Interview. *Women's Review of Books,* July/August 2006, http://www.wcwonline.org.

Sebbar, Leïla. *Je ne parle pas la langue de mon père.* Paris: Julliard, 2003.

———. *The Seine Was Red.* Trans. Mildred Mortimer. Bloomington: Indiana University Press, 2008. First published as *La Seine était rouge.* Paris: Thierry Magnier, 1999.

Shelton, Marie-Denise. "Haitian Women's Fiction." *Callaloo* 15.2 (1992): 770–77.

Stora, Benjamin. *La gangrène et l'oubli: La mémoire de la guerre d'Algérie.* Paris: La Découverte, 1991.

Tumarkin, Maria. *Traumascapes: The Power and Fate of Places Transformed by Tragedy.* Carleton: Melbourne University Press, 2005.

Walter, Victor. *Placeways: A Theory of the Human Environment.* Chapel Hill: University of North Carolina Press, 1988.